NAGUIB MAHFOUZ

The Thief and the Dogs

Naguib Mahfouz was one of the most prominent writers of Arabic fiction in the twentieth century. He was born in 1911 in Cairo and began writing at the age of seventeen. His first novel was published in 1939. Throughout his career, he wrote nearly forty novel-length works and hundreds of short stories. In 1988 Mr. Mahfouz was awarded the Nobel Prize in Literature. He died in 2006.

ALSO BY NAGUIB MAHFOUZ

*The Beggar**
*Autumn Quail**
The Beginning and the End
Wedding Song†
Respected Sir†
The Time and the Place and Other Stories
The Search†
Midaq Alley
The Journey of Ibn Fattouma
Miramar
Adrift on the Nile
The Harafish
Arabian Nights and Days
Children of the Alley
Echoes of an Autobiography
The Day the Leader Was Killed
Akhenaten, Dweller in Truth
Voices from the Other World
Rhadopis of Nubia
Khufu's Wisdom
The Seventh Heaven

The Cairo Trilogy:
Palace Walk
Palace of Desire
Sugar Street

*†published as omnibus editions

NAGUIB MAHFOUZ

The Thief and the Dogs

A Novel

Translated by Trevor Le Gassick and M. M. Badawi
Revised by John Rodenbeck

Anchor Books
A Division of Random House, Inc.
New York

ANCHOR BOOKS EDITION, JUNE 2008

 Published in the United States by Anchor Books, a division of Random House, Inc., New York, and in Canada by Random House of Canada Limited, Toronto. Originally published in Arabic as *Al-Lissa wa al-Kilab in* 1961. This English translation was first published by The American University in Cairo Press, Cairo and New York, in 1984.

This Anchor Books edition is published by arrangement with The American University in Cairo Press.

The Cataloging-in-Publication Data is on file at the Library of Congress.

Anchor ISBN: 978-0-385-26462-4

www.anchorbooks.com

Printed in the United States of America
10 9 8 7 6 5 4 3 2 1

INTRODUCTION

No writer of the modern Arab world has enjoyed a success in literature to approach that of Naguib Mahfouz. His work has become appreciated as a voluminous and sharply focused reflection of the Egyptian experience through the turbulent changes of the twentieth century. His fame within the Middle East is consequently unrivaled and the importance of his score of published works has been widely noted abroad. Many of his stories have previously appeared in English and other foreign languages and he has received honorary awards and degrees from Denmark, France, and the Soviet Union. His achievements are all the more extraordinary for his having remained employed full-time for over thirty years in various departments of the Egyptian civil service in which he reached administrative positions of importance before his retirement in 1972.

The work of Mahfouz, then, reveals many of the changes of aspiration and orientation of Egyptian intellectuals over the span of his lifetime. In the thirties, a time when Mahfouz was emerging from Cairo University with a degree in philosophy, Egyptians were struggling for equilibrium between the contradictory pulls of pride in Islam or in ancient Egypt. Their dilemma was compounded by their awareness of the attitude of foreigners toward their national heritage. They witnessed every day in the streets of Cairo the enthusiasm of archaeologists and tourists for the treasures of their ancient tombs and pyramids but they also knew of the glories of their religious, architectural, cultural, and, above all, language heritage from Islam and the Arabs. And they were only too aware of the disdain of foreigners for the state of their contemporary government and society.

Mahfouz's dilemma in orientation lasted, however, only for the thirties, during which he composed a rather strange medley of short stories dealing with the life of his own time and several works on the ancient history of his country. He translated an English text on ancient Egypt and wrote three historical novels depicting aspects of the lives and times of the pharaohs. In them his particular concern was for the relationships between rulers and the people and the uprising of the Egyptians against the Hyksos invaders, subjects of obvious interest to his readers critical of the despotic Egyptian monarchy under King Farouk, himself dominated by the strong British presence in the country. By the early forties, however, Mahfouz had abandoned his plan of constructing a massive series of novels based on ancient history and almost all his work since has related specifically to the Egypt that he has himself witnessed.

In that middle period of his work, then, he wrote a series of novels, first published obscurely and later to achieve great and continuing popularity, that dealt both with his own milieu, the Muslim middle-class of Cairo, and with that of the colorful characters of the conservative quarters of the ancient city. These were followed by his Cairo Trilogy, which caused a literary sensation in the late fifties and consequently drew attention back to his earlier works. A voluminous work, the Trilogy presents a detailed panorama of the life experiences of three generations of a Cairo merchant-class family over the turbulent first half of this century. It is a fascinating study of the social, political, religious, and philosophical strains experienced by his countrymen at that time of fast transition and the consequent effects on their personal relationships.

Following the 1952 Revolution of General Naguib and Colonel Nasser, Mahfouz wrote nothing for seven years. His 1959 *Awlad Haritna* (translated as *Children of Gebelawi*) was serialized in the daily newspaper *Al-Ahram* and never since republished in Egypt. It is a pessimistic portrayal in allegorical form of man's struggle for comprehension and solution of the problems of his existence. Discouraged by the furor the novel caused in traditional and religious circles, Mahfouz again refrained from writing for some time, until his publication of his present novel, *The Thief and the Dogs*, in 1961. This was well received and was followed by a stream of fine novels in the sixties that detailed with delicacy and great courage the crisis of identity and conscience suffered by Egyptian intellectuals during that period of pervasive malaise and dissatisfaction.

His more recent works, following the 1967 war with Israel, have been circumspect and philosophical and he has favored the short story and the short play for expression of his frequently allegorical themes. However, *Al-Hubb Tahta al-Matar (Love in the Rain)* published in mid-1973 in book form only, without serialization in the widely read daily press, contrasted (and by implication criticized) the free and at times immoral life which continued in Cairo with the soldiers' endless waiting, in discomfort and fear of death, for the inevitable renewal of warfare with Israel.

The present novel, then, was first published in 1961 and both its subject treatment and style marked distinct changes from Mahfouz's earlier work. This is a psychological novel, impressionist rather than realist; it moves with the speed and economy of a detective story. Here Mahfouz uses the stream-of-consciousness technique for the first time to show the mental anguish of his central figure consumed by bitterness and a desire for revenge against the individuals and the society who have corrupted and betrayed him and brought about his inevitable damnation. It is a masterly work, swiftly giving the reader a keenly accurate vision of the workings of a sick and embittered mind doomed to self-destruction. And as he inevitably comes to the protagonist's disillusionment and despair, the reader gains intimate and authentic impressions of the values and structures of Egyptian society of the period.

TREVOR LE GASSICK

The Thief and the Dogs

ONE

Once more he breathed the air of freedom. But there was stifling dust in the air, almost unbearable heat, and no one was waiting for him; nothing but his blue suit and gym shoes.

As the prison gate and its unconfessable miseries receded, the world—streets belabored by the sun, careening cars, crowds of people moving or still—returned.

No one smiled or seemed happy. But who of these people could have suffered more than he had, with four years lost, taken from him by betrayal? And the hour was coming when he would confront them, when his rage would explode and burn, when those who had betrayed him would despair unto death, when treachery would pay for what it had done.

Nabawiyya. Ilish. Your two names merge in my mind. For years you will have been thinking about this day, never imagining, all the while, that the gates would ever actually open. You'll be watching now, but I won't fall into the trap. At the right moment, instead, I'll strike like Fate.

And Sana? What about Sana?

As the thought of her crossed his mind, the heat and the dust, the hatred and pain all disappeared, leaving only love to glow across a soul as clear as a rain-washed sky.

I wonder how much the little one even knows about her father? Nothing, I suppose. No more than this road does, these passersby or this molten air.

She had never been out of his thoughts, where bit by bit she'd taken shape, like an image in a dream, for four long years. Would luck now give him some decent place to live, where such love could be equally shared, where he could take joy in being a winner again, where what Nabawiyya Ilish had done would be no more than a memory, odious, but almost forgotten?

You must pull together all the cunning you possess, to culminate in a blow as powerful as your endurance behind prison walls. Here is a man—a man who can dive like a fish, fly like a hawk, scale walls like a rat, pierce solid doors like a bullet!

How will he look when he first sees you? How will his eyes meet yours? Have you forgotten, Ilish, how you used to rub against my legs like a dog? It was me, wasn't it, who taught you how to stand on your own two feet, who made a man of a cigarette-butt cadger? You've forgotten, Ilish, and you're not the only one: She's forgotten, too, that woman who sprang from filth, from vermin, from treachery and infidelity.

Through all this darkness only your face, Sana, smiles. When we meet I'll know how I stand. In a little while, as soon as I've covered the length of this road, gone past all these gloomy arcades, where people used to have fun. Onward and upward. But not to glory. I swear I hate you all.

The bars have shut down and only the side streets are open, where plots are hatched. From time to time he has to cross over a hole in the pavement set there like a snare and the wheels of streetcars growl and shriek like abuse. *Confused cries seem to seep from the curbside garbage. (I swear I hate you all.) Houses of temptation, their windows beckoning even when eyeless, walls scowling where plaster has fallen. And that strange lane, al-Sayrafi Lane, which brings back dark memories. Where the thief stole, then vanished, whisked away. (Woe to the traitors.) Where police who'd staked out the area had slithered in to surround you.*

The same little street where a year before you'd been carrying home flour to make sweetmeats for the Feast, that woman walking in front of you, carrying Sana in her swaddling clothes. Glorious days—how real they were, no one knows—the Feast, love, parenthood, crime. All mixed up with this spot.

The great mosques and, beyond them, the Citadel against the clear sky, then the road flowing into the square, where the green park lies under the hot sun and a dry breeze blows, refreshing despite the heat—the Citadel square, with all its burning recollections.

What's important now is to make your face relax, to pour a little cold water over your feelings, to appear friendly and conciliatory, to play the planned role well. He crossed the middle of the square, entered Imam Way, and walked along it until he came close to the three-story house at the end, where two little streets joined the main road. *This social visit will tell you what they've got up their sleeves. So study the road carefully, and what's on it. Those shops, for instance, where the men are staring at you, cowering like mice.*

"Said Mahran!" said a voice behind him. "How marvelous!"

He let the man catch up with him; they said hello to each other, hiding their real feelings under mutual grins. *So the bastard has friends. He'll know right away what all these greetings are about. You're probably peeking at us through the shutters now, Ilish, hiding like a woman.*

"I thank you, Mr. Bayaza."

People came up to them from the shops on both sides of the street; voices were loud and warm in congratulation and Said found himself surrounded by a crowd—his enemy's friends, no doubt—who tried to outdo one another in cordiality.

"Thank God you're back safe and sound."

"All of us, your close friends, are overjoyed!"

"We all said we wished you'd be released on the anniversary of the Revolution."

"I thank God and you, gentlemen," he said, staring at them with his brown, almond-shaped eyes.

Bayaza patted him on the shoulder. "Come into the shop and have a cold drink to celebrate."

"Later," he said quietly. "When I'm back."

"Back?"

One man shouts, directing his voice to the second

story of the house: "Mr. Ilish! Mr. Ilish, come down and congratulate Said Mahran!" *No need to warn him, you black beetle! I've come in broad daylight. I know you've been watching.*

"Back from what?" said Bayaza.

"There's some business I have to settle."

"With whom?" said Bayaza.

"Have you forgotten I'm a father? And that my little girl's with Ilish?"

"No. But there's a solution to every disagreement. In the sacred law."

"And it's best to reach an understanding," said someone else.

"Said, you're fresh out of prison," a third man added in a conciliatory tone. "A wise man learns his lesson."

"Who said I'm here for anything other than to reach an understanding?"

On the second story of the building a window opened, Ilish leaned out, and they all looked up at him tensely. Before a word could be said, a big man wearing a striped garment and police boots came from the front door of the house. Said recognized Hasaballah, the detective, and pretended to be surprised.

"Don't get excited. I have come only to reach an amicable settlement," he said with feeling.

The detective came up and patted him all over, searching with practiced speed and skill. "Shut up, you cunning bastard. What did you say you wanted?"

"I've come to reach an understanding about the future of my daughter."

"As if you knew what understanding meant!"

"I do indeed, for my daughter's sake."

"You can always go to court."

Ilish shouted from above, "Let him come up. Come up all of you. You're all welcome." *Rally them round you, coward. I've only come to test the strength of your fortifications. When your hour arrives, neither detective nor walls will do you any good.*

They all crowded into a sitting room and planted themselves in sofas and chairs. The windows were opened: flies rushed in with the light. Cigarette burns had made black spots in the sky-blue carpet and from a large photograph on the wall Ilish, holding a thick stick with both his hands, stared out on the room. The detective sat next to Said and began to play with his worry beads.

Ilish Sidra came into the room, a loose garment swelling round his barrel-like body, his fat round face buttressed by a square chin. His huge nose had a broken bridge. "Thank the Lord you're back safe and sound!" he said, as if he had nothing to fear. But no one spoke, anxious looks passed back and forth, and the atmosphere was tense until Ilish continued: "What's over is done with, these things happen every day; unhappiness can occur, and old friendships often break up. But only shameful deeds can shame a man."

Conscious that his eyes were glittering, that he was slim and strong, Said felt like a tiger crouched to spring on an elephant. He found himself repeating Ilish's words: "Only shameful deeds can shame a man." Many eyes stared back at him; the detective's fingers stopped playing with his beads; realizing what was passing in their minds, he added as an afterthought, "I agree with every word you say."

"Come to the point," the detective broke in, "and stop beating about the bush."

"Which point?" Said said innocently.

"There's only one point to discuss, and that's your daughter."

And what about my wife and my fortune, you mangy dogs! I'll show you. Just wait. How I'd like to see now the look you'll have in your eyes. It would give me respect for beetles, scorpions, and worms, you vermin. Damn the man who lets himself be carried away by the melodious voice of woman. But Said nodded in agreement.

One of the sycophants said, "Your daughter is in safe hands with her mother. According to the law a six-year-old girl should stay with her mother. If you like, I could bring her to visit you every week."

Said raised his voice deliberately, so that he could be heard outside the room: "According to the law she should be in my custody. In view of the various circumstances."

"What do you mean?" Ilish said, suddenly angry.

"Arguing will only give you a headache," said the detective, trying to placate him.

"I have committed no crime. It was partly fate and circumstances, partly my sense of duty and decency that drove me to do what I did. And I did it partly for the sake of the little girl."

A sense of duty and decency, indeed, you snake! Double treachery, betrayal, and infidelity! Oh for the sledgehammer and the ax and the gallows rope! I wonder how Sana looks now. "I did not leave her in need," Said said, as calmly as he could. "She had my money, and plenty of it."

"You mean your loot," the detective roared, "the existence of which you denied in court!"

"All right, call it what you like. But where has it gone?"

"There wasn't a penny, believe me, friends!" Ilish protested loudly, "She was in a terrible predicament. I just did my duty."

"Then how have you been able to live in such comfort," Said challenged, "and spend so generously on others?"

"Are you God, that you should call me to account?"

"Peace, peace, shame the devil, Said," said one of Ilish's friends.

"I know you inside out, Said," the detective said slowly. "I can read your thoughts better than anyone. You will only destroy yourself. Just stick to the subject of the girl. That's the best thing for you."

Said looked down to hide his eyes, then smiled and said, in a tone of resignation, "You're quite right, Officer."

"I know you inside out. But I'll go along with you. Out of consideration for the people here. Bring the girl, someone. Wouldn't it be better to find out first what she thinks?"

"What do you mean, Officer?"

"Said, I know you. You don't want the girl. And you can't keep her, because you'll have difficulty enough finding some accommodation for yourself. But it's only fair and kind to let you see her. Bring in the girl."

Bring in her mother, you mean. How I wish our eyes could meet, so I might behold one of the secrets of hell! Oh for the ax and the sledgehammer!

Ilish went to fetch the girl. At the sound of returning footsteps Said's heart began to beat almost painfully, and as he stared at the door, he bit the inside of his lips, anticipation and tenderness stifling all his rage.

After what seemed a thousand years, the girl appeared. She looked surprised. She was wearing a smart white frock and white open slippers that showed henna-dyed toes. She gazed at him, her face dark, her black hair flowing over her forehead, while his soul devoured her. Bewildered, she looked around at all the other faces, then particularly at his, which was staring so intently. He was unable to take his eyes off her. As she felt herself being pushed toward him, she planted her feet on the carpet and leaned backward away from him. And suddenly he felt crushed by a sense of total loss.

It was as if, in spite of her almond-shaped eyes, her long face, and her slender, aquiline nose, she was not his own daughter. Where were the instinctive ties of blood and soul? Were they, too, treacherous, deceptive? And how could he, even so, resist the almost overwhelming desire to hug her to him forever?

"This is your father, child," said the detective impatiently.

"Shake hands with Daddy," said Ilish, his face impassive.

She's like a mouse. What's she afraid of? Doesn't she know how much I love her? He stretched out his hand toward her, but instead of being able to say anything he had a fit of choking and had to swallow hard, managing only to smile at her tenderly, invitingly.

"No!" said Sana. She backed away, trying to steal out of the room, but a man standing behind stopped her. "Mommy!" she cried, but the man pushed her gently and said, "Shake hands with Daddy." Everyone looked on with malicious interest.

Said knew now that prison lashings had not been as cruel as he used to think. "Come to me, Sana," he pleaded, unable to bear her refusal any longer, half standing and drawing closer to her.

"No!" she shouted.

"I am your daddy." She raised her eyes to Ilish Sidra in bewilderment, but Said repeated emphatically, "I am your daddy, come to me." She shrank back even further. He pulled her toward him almost forcibly. Then she screamed, and as he drew her closer, she fought back, crying. He leaned forward to kiss her, disregarding his failure and disappointment, but his lips caught only a whirling arm. "I'm your daddy. Don't be afraid. I'm your dad." The scent on her hair filled his mind with the memory of her mother; he felt his face go hard. The child struggled and wept more violently, and finally the detective intervened: "Easy, easy, the child does not know you."

Defeated, Said let her run away. "I will take her," he said angrily, sitting bolt upright.

A moment of silence passed, at the end of which Bayaza said, "Calm yourself first."

"She must come back to me."

"Let the judge decide that," the detective said sharply, then turned questioningly to Ilish. "Yes?"

"It has nothing to do with me. Her mother will never give her up, except in compliance with the law."

"Just as I pointed out at the beginning. There's no more to be said. It's up to a court of law."

Said felt that if once given vent, his rage would be unrestrainable and therefore with supreme effort he managed to keep it under control, reminding himself of things he had almost forgotten. "Yes, the court of law," he said as calmly as he could.

"And as you can see, the girl is being very well looked after," said Bayaza.

"First find yourself an honest job," the detective said with an ironic smile.

Able now to control himself, Said said, "Yes, of course. All that's quite correct. No need to be upset. I'll reconsider the whole affair. The best thing would be to forget the past and start looking for a job to provide a suitable home for the child when the time comes."

During the surprised silence that followed this speech, glances were exchanged, some incredulous, some perhaps not. The detective gathered his worry beads into his fist and asked, "Are we finished now?"

"Yes," Said answered. "I only want my books."

"Your books?"

"Yes."

"Most of them have been lost by Sana," Ilish said loudly, "but I'll bring you whatever is left." He disappeared for a few minutes and returned carrying a modest pile of books, which he deposited in the middle of the room.

Said leafed through them, picking up one volume after another. "Yes," he remarked sadly, "most of them have been lost."

"How did you acquire all this learning?" the detective said with a laugh, rising to signal the end of the meeting. "Did you steal reading matter as well?"

They all grinned except Said, who went out carrying his books.

TWO

He looked at the door, open as it always used to be, as he walked up Jabal Road toward it. Here, enclosed by ridges of the Muqattam hill, was the Darrasa quarter, the scene of so many pleasant memories. The sandy ground was dotted with animals, teeming with children. Said gazed delightedly at the little girls panting from both emotion and exhaustion. Men lolled around him in the shade of the hill, away from the declining sun.

At the threshold of the open door he paused, trying to remember when he'd crossed it last. The simplicity of the house, which could hardly be different from those of Adam's day, was striking. At the left corner of the big, open courtyard stood a tall palm tree with a crooked top; to the right an entrance corridor led by an open door—in this strange house no door was ever closed—to a single room. His heart beat fast, carrying him back to a distant, gentle time of childhood, dreams, a loving father, and his own innocent yearning. He recalled the men filling the courtyard, swaying with their chanting, God's praise echoing from the depths of their hearts. "Look and listen, learn and open your heart," his father used to say. Besides a joy like the joy of Paradise that was aroused in him by faith and dreams, there had also been the joy of singing and green tea. He wondered how Ali al-Junaydi was.

From inside the room he could hear a man concluding his prayers. Said smiled, slipped in carrying his books, and saw the Sheikh sitting cross-legged on the prayer carpet, absorbed in quiet recitation. The old room had hardly changed. The rush mats had been replaced by new ones, thanks to his disciples, but the Sheikh's sleeping mattress still lay close to the western wall, pierced by a window through which the rays of the declining sun were pouring down at Said's feet. The other walls of the room were half covered with rows of books on shelves. The odor of incense lingered as if it were the same he remembered, never dissipated, from years ago. Putting down his load of books, he approached the Sheikh.

"Peace be upon you, my lord and master."

Having completed his recitation, the Sheikh raised his head, disclosing a face that was emaciated but radiant with overflowing vitality, framed by a white beard like a halo, and surmounted by a white skullcap that nestled in thick locks of hair showing silvery at his temples. The Sheikh scrutinized him with eyes that had been viewing this world for eighty years and indeed had glimpsed the next, eyes that had not lost their appeal, acuteness, or charm. Said found himself bending over his hand to kiss it, suppressing tears of nostalgia for his father, his boyish hopes, the innocent purity of the distant past.

"Peace and God's compassion be upon you," said the Sheikh in a voice like Time.

What had his father's voice been like? He could see his father's face and his lips moving, and tried to make his eyes do the service of ears, but the voice had gone. And the disciples, the men chanting the mystical *dhikr*, "O master, the Prophet is at your gate!"—where were they now?

He sat down cross-legged on the rush mat before the Sheikh. "I am sitting without asking your permission," he said. "I remember that you prefer that." He sensed that the Sheikh was smiling, though on those lips concealed amidst the whiteness, no smile was visible. Did the Sheikh remember him? "Forgive my coming to your house like this. But there's nowhere else in the world for me to go."

The Sheikh's head drooped to his breast. "You seek the walls, not the heart," he whispered.

Said was baffled; not knowing what to say, he sighed, then quietly remarked, "I got out of jail today."

"Jail?" said the Sheikh, his eyes closed.

"Yes. You haven't seen me for more than ten years, and during that time strange things have happened to me. You've probably heard about them from some of your disciples who know me."

"Because I hear much I can hardly hear anything."

"In any case, I didn't want to meet you under false pretenses, so I'm telling you I got out of jail only today."

The Sheikh slowly shook his head, then, opening his eyes, said, "You have not come from jail." The voice was sorrowful.

Said smiled. This was the language of old times again, where words had a double meaning.

"Master, every jail is tolerable, except the government jail."

The Sheikh glanced at him with clear and lucid eyes, then muttered, "He says every jail is tolerable except the government jail."

Said smiled again, though he'd almost given up hope of being able to communicate, and asked, "Do you remember me?"

"Your concern is the present hour."

Fairly certain that he was remembered, Said asked for reassurance: "And do you remember my father, Mr. Mahran, God have mercy upon his soul?"

"May God have mercy upon all of us."

"What wonderful days those were!"

"Say that, if you can, about the present."

"But . . ."

"God have mercy upon us all."

"I was saying, I just got out of jail today."

The Sheikh nodded his head, showing sudden vigor. "And as he was impaled on the stake he smiled and said, 'It was God's will that I should meet Him thus.' "

My father could understand you. But me you turned away from, treating me as if you were turning me out of your house. And even so I've come back here, of my own accord, to this atmosphere of incense and disquiet, because a man so desolate, with no roof over his head, cannot do otherwise.

"Master, I have come to you now when my own daughter has rejected me."

The Sheikh sighed. "God reveals His secrets to His tiniest creatures!"

"I thought that if God had granted you long life, I would find your door open."

"And the door of Heaven? How have you found that?"

"But there is nowhere on earth for me to go. And my own daughter has rejected me."

"How like you she is!"

"In what way, Master?"

"You seek a roof, not an answer."

Said rested his head with its short, wiry hair on his dark, thin hand, and said, "My father used to seek you out when he was in trouble, so I found myself . . ."

"You seek a roof and nothing else."

Convinced that the Sheikh knew who he was, Said felt uneasy but did not know why. "It's not only a roof," he said. "I want more than that. I would like to ask God to be pleased with me."

The Sheikh replied as if intoning. "The celestial Lady said, 'Aren't you ashamed to ask for His good pleasure while you are not well pleased with Him?' "

The open space outside resounded with the braying of a donkey, which ended in a throaty rattle like a sob. Somewhere a harsh voice was singing, "Where have luck and good fortune gone?" He remembered once when his father had caught him singing "I Give You Three Guesses": his father had punched him gently and said, "Is this an appropriate song on our way to the blessed Sheikh?" He remembered how, in the midst of the chanting, his father had reeled in ecstasy, his eyes swimming, his voice hoarse, sweat pouring down his face, while he himself sat at the foot of the palm tree, watching the disciples by the light of a lantern, nibbling a fruit, rapt in curious bliss. All that was before he'd felt the first scalding drop of the draught of love.

The Sheikh's eyes were closed now, as if he were asleep, and Said had become so adjusted to the setting and atmosphere that he could no longer smell the incense. It occurred to him that habit is the root of laziness, boredom, and death, that habit had been responsible for his sufferings, the treachery, the ingratitude, and the waste of his life's hard toil. "Are the *dhikr* meetings still held here?" he asked, attempting to rouse the Sheikh.

But the Sheikh gave no answer. Even more uneasy now, Said asked a further question: "Aren't you going to welcome me here?"

The Sheikh opened his eyes and said, "Weak are the seeker and the sought."

"But you are the master of the house."

"The Owner of the house welcomes you," the Sheikh said, suddenly jovial, "as He welcomes every creature and every thing." Encouraged, Said smiled, but the Sheikh added, as if it were an afterthought, "As for me, I am master of nothing."

The sunlight on the rush mat had retreated to the wall.

"In any case," said Said, "this house is my real home, as it always was a home for my father and for every supplicant. You, my Master, deserve all our gratitude."

" 'Lord, you know how incapable I am of doing You justice in thanking you, so please thank yourself on my account!' Thus spake one of the grateful."

"I am in need of a kind word," Said pleaded.

"Do not tell lies." The Sheikh spoke gently, then bowed his head, his beard fanning out over his chest, and seemed lost in thought.

Said waited, then shifted backward to rest against one of the bookshelves, where for several minutes he sat contemplating the fine-looking old man, until finally impatience made him ask, "Is there anything I could do for you?"

The Sheikh did not bother to respond and a period of silence followed, during which Said watched a line of ants nimbly crawling along a fold in the mat. Suddenly the Sheikh said, "Take a copy of the Koran and read."

A little confused, Said explained apologetically, "I just got out of jail today, and I have not performed the prayer ablutions."

"Wash yourself now and read."

"My own daughter has rejected me. She was scared

of me, as if I was the devil. And before that her mother was unfaithful to me."

"Wash and read," replied the Sheikh gently.

"She committed adultery with one of my men, a layabout, a mere pupil of mine, utterly servile. She applied for divorce on grounds of my imprisonment and went and married him."

"Wash and read."

"And he took everything I owned, the money and the jewelry. He's a big man now, and all the local crooks have become followers and cronies of his."

"Wash and read."

"It wasn't thanks to any sweat by the police that I was arrested." Said went on, the veins in his forehead pulsing with anger. "No, it wasn't. I was sure of my safety, as usual. It was that dog who betrayed me, in collusion with her. Then disaster followed disaster until finally my daughter rejected me."

"Wash and read the verses: 'Say to them: if you love God, then follow me and God will love you' and 'I have chosen thee for Myself.' Also repeat the words: 'Love is acceptance, which means obeying His commands and refraining from what He has prohibited and contentment with what He decrees and ordains.' "

I could see my father listening and nodding his head with pleasure, looking at me with a smile as if saying: "Listen and learn." I had been happy then, hoping no one could see me, so I could climb the palm tree or throw up a stone to bring down a date, singing to myself along with those chant-

ing men. Then one evening when I'd come back to the students' hostel in Giza I saw her coming towards me, holding a basket, pretty and charming, all the joys of heaven and torments of hell that I was fated to experience hidden within her.

What had it been about the chanting I'd liked, when they recited: "As soon as He appeared the beacon of faith shone" and: "I saw the crescent moon and the face of the beloved"? But the sun is not yet set. The last golden thread is receding from the window. A long night is waiting for me, the first night of freedom. I am alone with my freedom, or rather I'm in the company of the Sheikh, who is lost in heaven, repeating words that cannot be understood by someone approaching hell. What other refuge have I?

THREE

Flipping eagerly through the pages of *Al-Zahra* until he found Rauf Ilwan's column, Said began to read while still only a few yards from the house where he'd spent the night, the house of Sheikh Ali al-Junaydi. But what was it that seemed to be inspiring Ilwan now? Said found only comments on women's fashions, on loudspeakers, and a reply to a complaint by an anonymous wife. Diverting enough, but what had become of the Rauf Ilwan he'd known? Said thought of the good old days at the students' hostel, and particularly of the wonderful enthusiasm that had radiated from a young peasant with shabby clothes, a big heart, and a direct and glittering style of writing. What was it that had happened in the world? What lay behind these strange and mysterious events? Did things happen that were similar to what took place in al-Sayrafi Lane? And how about Nabawiyya and Ilish and that dear little girl who rejected her father? I must see him, he thought. The Sheikh has given me a mat to sleep on; but I need money. *I must begin life afresh, Mr. Ilwan, and for that purpose you are no less important than Sheikh Ali. You are, in fact, the most important thing I have in this insecure world.*

He walked on until he reached the *Zahra* offices in Maarif Square, an enormous building, where his first thought was that it would be very difficult to break into. The rows of cars surrounding it were like guards around a prison; the rumble of printing presses behind the grilles of the basement windows was like the low hum of men sleeping in a dormitory. He joined the stream of people entering the building, presented himself at the information desk, and asked in his deep "public" voice for Mr. Rauf Ilwan. Staring back with some displeasure at the bold, almost impudent look in his eyes, the reception clerk snapped, "Fourth floor." Said made for the elevator at once, joining people among whom he looked rather out of place in his blue suit and gym shoes, the oddness emphasized by the glaring eyes on either side of his long aquiline nose. A girl caught his eye, which made him curse his ex-wife and her lover under his breath, promising them destruction.

From the corridor of the fourth floor he slipped into the secretary's office before an attendant had time to intercept him and found himself in a large rectangular room with one glass wall overlooking the street, but no place to sit. He heard the secretary on the telephone, telling someone that Mr. Rauf was at a meeting with the editor-in-chief and would not be back for at least two hours. Feeling alien and out of place, Said poised himself with bravado, staring at the other people in the room almost defiantly, remembering a time when he would have fixed his gaze on people like them as if he wished to cut their throats. What were such people like nowadays? he wondered.

Rauf was now a very important man, it seemed, a great man, as great as this room. It isn't a suitable place for reunion of old friends. Rauf won't be able to behave naturally here. There was a time when he'd been nothing more than a scribbler with the magazine *Al-Nadhir*, tucked away in Sharia Muhammad Ali, a poor writer whose voice rang with demands for freedom. *I wonder what you're like now, Rauf? Will he have changed, like you, Nabawiyya? Will he disown me, as Sana has done? No, I must banish these evil thoughts. He's still a friend and mentor, a sword of freedom ever drawn, and he'll always be like that, despite this impressiveness, this plush office suite, and those puzzling articles. If this citadel will not allow me to embrace you, Rauf, I'll have to look in the telephone directory and find your home address.*

Seated on the damp grass along the riverbank beside Sharia al-Nil, he waited. He waited even longer near a tree silhouetted by the light of an electric lamp. The crescent moon had gone down early, leaving stars to glitter in a sky profoundly black, and a soft breeze blew, distilled from the breath of the night after a day of stunning, searing summer. There he sat, with his arms clasped around his knees and his back to the river, his eyes fixed on villa number 18.

What a palace, he thought. It was open on three sides, and an extensive garden lay on the fourth. The trees stood around the white body of the building like whispering figures. A scene like this felt familiar, full of reminders of the good living he'd once enjoyed. How had Rauf managed it? And in such a short time! Not even thieves could dream of owning a thing like this. *I never used to look at a villa like this except when I was making plans to break into it. Is there really any hope of finding friendship in such a place now? You are indeed a mystery, Rauf Ilwan, and you must be made to reveal your secret.*

Wasn't it strange that Ilwan rhymed with Mahran? And that that dog Ilish should grab and wallow in the fruits of my lifetime's labor?

When a car stopped in front of the villa gate he sprang to his feet. As the porter opened the gate he darted across the road and stood before the car, bending a little so the driver could see him. When the man inside apparently failed to recognize him in the dark, Said roared, "Mr. Rauf, I am Said Mahran." The man put his head close to the open window of the car and repeated his name, in obvious surprise, his low voice carefully modulated. Said could not read Rauf's expression, but the tone of voice was encouraging. After a moment of silence and inaction, the car door opened and Said heard him say, "Get in."

A good beginning, he thought. Rauf Ilwan was the same man he knew, despite the glass-filled office suite and the lovely villa. The car went down a drive that curved like the shape of a violin, toward a flight of steps leading to the main entrance of the house.

"How are you, Said? When did you get out?"

"Yesterday."

"Yesterday?"

"Yes, I should have come to see you, but I had some things I had to attend to and I needed rest, so I spent the night at Sheikh Ali al-Junaydi's. Remember him?"

"Sure. Your late father's Sheikh. I watched his meetings with you lots of times." They left the car and went into the reception hall.

"They were fun, weren't they?"

"Yes, and I used to get a big kick out of their singing."

A servant switched on the chandelier, and Said's eyes were dazzled by its size, its multitude of upturned bulbs, its stars and crescents. The light that spread throughout the room was caught in mirrors at the corners, reflecting the brilliance. Objets d'art on gilt stands were displayed as if they had been salvaged from the obscurity of history for that sole purpose. The ceiling, he saw, was richly decorated, while all around him comfortable chairs and cushions were casually disposed among vividly patterned carpets. His eyes rested last on the face of Maître Ilwan, now round and full, a face he had loved, whose features he had long ago learned by heart, having gazed at it so often while listening to Rauf speak; and stealing occasional glances at the objets d'art, Said went on examining that face while a servant drew back curtains and opened French windows to the veranda overlooking the garden, letting a breeze heavy with the perfume of blossomy trees flow into the room.

The mixture of light and scent was distracting, but Said observed that Ilwan's face had become cowlike in its fullness, and that despite his apparent friendliness and courtesy, there was something chilly about him, as well as an unfamiliar and rather disturbing suavity, a quality that could only have come from a touch of blue blood, despite Rauf's flat nose and heavy jaw. What refuge would be left if this only surviving support also collapsed?

Rauf sat near the French windows to the veranda on a sofa that was arranged with three easy chairs in a square around a luminous pillar adorned with mythological figures. Said sat down, without hesitation and without showing his anxiety.

Ilwan stretched out his long legs. "Did you look for me at the paper?"

"Yes, but I saw it wasn't a suitable place for us to meet."

Rauf laughed, showing teeth stained black at the gums. "The office is like a whirlpool, in constant motion. Have you been waiting long here?"

"A lifetime!"

Rauf laughed again. "There was a time no doubt when you were quite familiar with this street?"

"Of course." Said, too, laughed. "My business transactions with my clients here made their premises unforgettable. The villa of Fadil Hasanayn Pasha, for instance, where my visit netted a thousand pounds, or the one that belongs to the film star Kawakib, where I got a pair of superb diamond earrings."

The servant came in pushing a trolley laden with a bottle, two glasses, a pretty little violet-colored ice bucket, a dish of apples arranged in a pyramid, plates with hors d'oeuvres, and a silver water jug.

Rauf gestured to the servant to withdraw, filled two glasses himself and offered one to Said, raising the other: "To freedom." While Said emptied his glass in one gulp, Rauf took a sip and then said, "And how is your daughter? Oh, I forgot to ask you—why did you spend the night at Sheikh Ali's?"

He doesn't know what happened, thought Said, but he still remembers my daughter. And he gave Rauf a cold-blooded account of his misfortunes.

"So yesterday I paid a visit to al-Sayrafi Lane," he concluded. "There I found a detective waiting for me, as I'd expected, and my daughter disowned me and screamed in my face." He helped himself to another whiskey.

"This is a sad story. But your daughter isn't to blame. She can't remember you now. Later on she'll grow to know and love you."

"I have no faith left in all her sex."

"That's how you feel now. But tomorrow, who knows how you'll feel? You'll change your opinion of your own accord. That's the way of the world."

The telephone rang. Rauf rose, picked up the receiver and listened for a moment. His face began to beam and he carried the telephone outside to the veranda, while Said's sharp eyes registered everything. It must be a woman. A smile like that, strolling into the dark, could only mean a woman. He wondered if Ilwan was still unmarried. Though they sat there cozily drinking and chatting, Said now sensed that this meeting would be exceedingly difficult to repeat. The feeling was unaccountable, like the whispered premonition of some still undiagnosed cancerous growth, but he trusted it, relying on instinct. A resident now in one of those streets that Said had only visited as a burglar, this man after all, may have felt obliged to welcome him, having actually changed so much that only a shadow of the old self remained. When Said heard Rauf's sudden laugh resounding on the veranda, he felt even less reassured. Calmly, however, he took an apple and began to munch it, pondering the extent to which his whole life had been no more than the mere acting out of ideas that had come from that man now chuckling into a telephone. What if Rauf should prove to have betrayed those ideas?

He would then have to pay dearly for it. On that score there was not the slightest doubt.

Rauf Ilwan came in from the veranda, replaced the telephone, and sat down looking extremely pleased. "So. Congratulations on your freedom. Being free is precious indeed. It more than makes up for losing anything else, no matter how valuable." Helping himself to a slice of pastrami, Said nodded in agreement, but without real interest in what had just been said.

"And now you've come out of prison to find a new world," Rauf went on, refilling both glasses while Said wolfed down the hors d'oeuvres.

Glancing at his companion, Said caught a look of disgust, quickly covered by a smile. You must be mad to think he was sincere in welcoming you. This is only superficial courtesy—doing the right thing—and will evaporate. Every kind of treachery pales beside this; what a void would then swallow up the entire world!

Rauf stretched his hand to a cigarette box, adorned with Chinese characters, placed in a hollow in the illuminated pillar. "My dear Said," he said, taking a cigarette, "everything that used to spoil life's pleasures for us has now completely disappeared."

"The news astounded us in prison," Said said, his mouth full of food. "Who could have predicted such things?" He looked at Rauf, smiling. "No class war now?"

"Let there be a truce! Every struggle has its proper field of battle."

"And this magnificent drawing room," said Said, looking around him, "is like a parade ground." He saw a cold look in his companion's eyes and regretted the words instantly. Why can't your tongue ever learn to be polite?

"What do you mean?" Rauf's voice was icy.

"I mean it's a model of sophisticated taste and—"

"Don't try to be evasive," said Rauf with narrowed

eyes. "Out with it. I understand you perfectly, I know you better than anybody else."

Said attempted a disarming laugh, then said, "I meant no harm at all."

"Never forget that I live by the sweat of my brow."

"I haven't doubted that for a moment. Please don't be angry."

Rauf puffed hard on his cigarette but made no further comment.

Aware that he ought to stop eating, Said said apologetically, "I haven't quite got over the atmosphere of prison. I need some time to recover my good manners and learn polite conversation. Apart from the fact that my head's still spinning from that strange meeting, when my own daughter rejected me."

Rauf's Mephistophelean eyebrows lifted in what looked like silent forgiveness. When he saw Said's gaze wander from his face to the food, as if asking permission to resume eating, he said quite calmly. "Help yourself."

Said attacked the rest of the dishes without hesitation, as if nothing had happened, until he'd wiped them clean. At this point Rauf said, a little quickly, as if he wished to end the meeting, "Things must now change completely. Have you thought about your future?"

Said lit a cigarette. "My past hasn't yet allowed me to consider the future."

"It occurs to me that there are more women in the

world than men. So you mustn't let the infidelity of one lone female bother you. As for your daughter, she'll get to know you and love you one day. The important thing now is to look for a job."

Said eyed a statue of a Chinese god, a perfect embodiment of dignity and repose. "I learned tailoring in prison."

"So you want to set up a tailoring shop?" said Rauf with surprise.

"Certainly not," Said replied quietly.

"What then?"

Said looked at him. "In my whole life I've mastered only one trade."

"You're going back to burglary?" Rauf seemed almost alarmed.

"It's most rewarding, as you know."

"As I know! How the hell do I know?"

"Why are you so angry?" Said gave him a surprised look. "I meant: as you know from my past. Isn't that so?"

Rauf lowered his eyes as if trying to assess the sincerity of Said's remark, clearly unable to maintain his bonhomie and looking for a way to end the meeting. "Listen, Said. Things are no longer what they used to be. In the past you were both a thief and my friend, for reasons you well know. Now the situation has changed. If you go back to burglary you'll be a thief and nothing else."

Dashed by Rauf's unaccommodating frankness,

Said sprang to his feet. Then he stifled his agitation, sat down again, and said quietly, "All right. Name a job that's suitable for me."

"Any job, no matter what. You do the talking. I'll listen."

"I would be happy," Said began, without obvious irony, "to work as a journalist on your paper. I'm a well-educated man and an old disciple of yours. Under your supervision I've read countless books, and you often testified to my intelligence."

Rauf shook his head impatiently, his thick black hair glistening in the brilliant light "This is no time for joking. You've never been a writer, and you got out of jail only yesterday. This fooling around is wasting my time."

"So I have to choose something menial?"

"No job is menial, as long as it's honest."

Said felt utterly reckless. He ran his eyes quickly over the smart drawing room, then said bitterly, "How marvelous it is for the rich to recommend poverty to us." Rauf's reaction was to look at his watch.

"I am sure I have taken too much of your time," Said said quietly.

"Yes," said Rauf, with all the blank directness of a July sun. "I'm loaded with work!"

"Thanks for your kindness and hospitality and for the supper," Said said, standing up.

Rauf took out his wallet and handed him two five-pound notes. "Take these to tide you over. Please forgive me for saying I'm overloaded with work. You'll seldom find me free as I was tonight."

Said smiled, took the bank notes, shook his hand warmly, and wished him well: "May God increase your good fortune."

FOUR

So this is the real Rauf Ilwan, the naked reality—a partial corpse not even decently undergound. The other Rauf Ilwan has gone, disappeared, like yesterday, like the first day in the history of man—like Nabawiyya's love or Ilish's loyalty. I must not be deceived by appearances. His kind words are cunning, his smiles no more than a curl of the lips, his generosity a defensive flick of the fingers, and only a sense of guilt moved him to let me cross the threshold of his house. You made me and now you reject me: Your ideas create their embodiment in my person and then you simply change them, leaving me lost—rootless, worthless, without hope—a betrayal so vile that if the whole Muqattam hill toppled over and buried it, I still would not be satisfied.

I wonder if you ever admit, even to yourself, that you betrayed me. Maybe you've deceived yourself as much as you try to deceive others. Hasn't your conscience bothered you even in the dark? I wish I could penetrate your soul as easily as I've penetrated your house, that house of mirrors and objets d'art, but I suppose I'd find nothing but betrayal there: Nabawiyya disguised as Rauf, Rauf disguised as Nabawiyya, or Ilish Sidra in place of both—and betrayal would cry out to me that it was the lowest crime on earth. Their eyes behind my back must have traded anxious looks throbbing with lust, which carried them in a current crawling like death, like a cat creeping on its belly toward a bewildered sparrow. When their chance came, the last remnants of decency and indecision disappeared, so that in a corner of the lane, even in my own house, Ilish Sidra finally said, "I'll tell the police. We'll get rid of him," and the child's mother was silent—the tongue that so often and so profusely told me, "I love you, the best man in the world," was silent. And I found myself surrounded by police in Al-Sayrafi Lane—though until then demons themselves with all their wiles had failed to trap me—their kicks and punches raining down on me.

You're just the same, Rauf—I don't know which of you is the most treacherous—except that your guilt is greater because of your intelligence and the past association between us: You pushed me into jail, while you leapt free, into that palace of lights and mirrors. You've forgotten your wise sayings about palaces and hovels, haven't you? I will never forget.

At the Abbas Bridge, sitting on a stone bench, he became aware for the first time of where he was.

"It's best to do it now," he said in a loud voice, as if addressing the dark, "before he's had time to get over the shock." I can't hold back, he thought. My profession will always be mine, a just and legitimate trade, especially when it's directed against its own philosopher. There'll be space enough in the world to hide after I've punished the bastards. If I could live without a past, ignoring Nabawiyya, Ilish, and Rauf, I'd be relieved of a great weight, a burden; I'd feel readier to secure an easy life and a lot further from the rope. But unless I settle my account with them, life will have no taste, because I shall not forget the past. For the simple reason that in my mind it's not a past, but the here and now. Tonight's adventure will be the best beginning for my program of action. And it'll be a rich venture indeed.

The Nile flowed in black waves slashed sidelong by arrows of light from the reflected streetlamps along its banks. The silence was soothing and total.

At the approach of dawn, as the stars drew closer to earth, Said rose from his seat, stretched, and began to walk slowly back along the bank toward the place from which he'd come, avoiding the few still-lit lamps, slowing his steps even more when the house came in sight. Examining the street, the terrain, the walls of the big houses as well as the riverbank, his eyes finally came to rest on the sleeping villa, guarded on all sides by trees like ghostly figures, where treachery dozed in a fine unmerited tranquillity. *It's going to be a rich venture, indeed, and one to give an emphatic reply to the treachery of a lifetime.*

He crossed the street casually without a movement to either right or left, without looking wary. Then followed the hedge down a side street, scanning carefully ahead. When he was sure the street was empty he dodged into the hedge, forcing his way in amidst the jasmine and violets, and stood motionless: If there was a dog in the house—other than its owner, of course—it would now fill the universe with barking.

But not a whisper came out of the silence.

Rauf, your pupil is coming, to relieve you of a few worldly goods.

He climbed the hedge nimbly, his expert limbs agile as an ape's, undeterred by the thick, intertwining branches, the heavy foliage and flowers. Gripping the railings, he heaved his body up over the sharp-pointed spikes, then lowered himself until his legs caught the branches inside the garden. Here he clung for a while regaining his breath, studying the terrain: a jungle of bushes, trees, and dark shadows. *I'll have to climb up to the roof and find a way to get in and down. I have no tools, no flashlight, no good knowledge of the house: Nabawiyya hasn't been here before me pretending to work as a washerwoman or a maid; she's busy now with Ilish Sidra.*

Scowling in the dark, trying to chase these thoughts from his mind, he dropped lightly to the ground. Crawling up to the villa on all fours, he felt his way along a wall until he found a drainpipe. Then, gripping it like an acrobat, he began to climb toward the roof. Partway up he spotted an open window, just out of reach, and decided to try it. He steered one foot to the window ledge, and shifted his hands, one at a time, to grip a cornice. Finally, when he could stand with his whole weight, he slid inside, finding himself in what he guessed was the kitchen. The dense darkness was disturbing and he groped for the door. The darkness would be even thicker inside, but where else could he find Rauf's wallet or some of his objets d'art? He had to go on.

Slipping through the door, feeling along the wall with his hands, he had covered a considerable distance, almost deterred by the darkness, when he felt a slight draft touch his face. Wondering where it could come from, he turned a corner and crept along the smooth wall, his arm stretched out, feeling ahead with his fingers. Suddenly they brushed some dangling beads, which rustled slightly as he touched them, making him start. A curtain. He must now be near his goal. He thought of the box of matches in his pocket, but instead of reaching for it he made a quiet little opening for himself in the hanging beads and slipped through, bringing the curtain back into position behind him, slowly, to avoid making any sound. He took one step forward and bumped some object, perhaps a chair, which he edged away from, raising his head to look for a night light. All he could see was a darkness that weighed down upon him like a nightmare. For a moment he thought again of lighting a match.

Suddenly he was assailed by light. It shone all around him, so powerful that it struck him with the force of a blow, making him shut his eyes. When he opened them again, Rauf Ilwan was standing only a couple of yards from him, wearing a long dressing gown, which made him look like a giant, one hand tensed in a pocket, as if he was clutching a weapon. The cold look in his eyes, his tightly closed lips, chilled Said to the core; nothing but deep hatred, hostility. The silence was suffocating, claustrophobic, denser than the walls of a prison. Abd Rabbuh the jailer would soon be jeering: "Back already?"

"Should we call the police?" someone behind him said curtly. Said turned around and saw three servants standing in a row. "Wait outside," said Rauf, breaking the silence.

As the door opened and closed Said observed that it was made of wood in arabesque designs, its upper panel inlaid with an inscription, probably a proverb or a Koranic verse. He turned to face Rauf.

"It was idiotic of you to try your tricks on me; I know you. I can read you like an open book." Speechless, helpless, and resigned, still recovering from the shock of surprise, Said had nevertheless an instinctive sense that he would not be handed back to the custody from which he'd been set free the day before. "I've been waiting for you, fully prepared. In fact, I even drew up your plan of action. I'd hope my expectation would be disappointed. But evidently no mistrust in you can prove groundless." Said lowered his eyes for a moment and became aware of the patterned parquet beneath the wax on the floor. Then he looked up, saying nothing. "It's no use. You'll always be worthless and you'll die a worthless death. The best thing I can do now is hand you over to the police." Said blinked, gulped, and lowered his eyes again.

"What have you come for?" Rauf demanded angrily. "You treat me as an enemy. You've forgotten my kindness, my charity. You feel nothing but malice and envy. I know your thoughts, as clearly as I know your actions."

His eyes still wandering over the floor, Said muttered, "I feel dizzy. Peculiar. It's been like that ever since I got out of jail."

"Liar! Don't try to deceive me. You thought I'd become one of the rich I used to attack. And with that in mind you wished to treat me—"

"It's not true."

"Then why did you break into my house? Why do you want to rob me?"

"I don't know," Said said, after a moment's hesitation. "I'm not in my proper state of mind. But you don't believe me."

"Of course I don't. You know you're lying. My good advice didn't persuade you. Your envy and arrogance were aroused, so you rushed in headlong as always, like a madman. Suit yourself, do what you like, but you'll find yourself in jail again."

"Please forgive me. My mind's the way it was in prison, the way it was even before that."

"There's no forgiving you. I can read your thoughts, everything that passes through your mind. I can see exactly what you think of me. And now it's time I delivered you to the police."

"Please don't."

"No? Don't you deserve it?"

"Yes, I do, but please don't."

"If I set eyes on you again," Rauf bellowed, "I'll squash you like an insect." Thus dismissed, Said was about to make a quick exit, but Rauf stopped him with a shout: "Give me back the money." Frozen for a second, Said slipped his hand into his pocket and brought out the two bank notes. Rauf took them and said, "Don't ever show me your face again."

Said walked back to the banks of the Nile, hardly believing his escape, though relief was spoiled by a sense of defeat, and now in the damp breath of early daybreak, he wondered how he could have failed to take careful note of the room where he'd been caught, how all he'd noticed had been its decorated door and its waxed parquet. But the dawn shed dewy compassion, giving momentary solace for the loss of everything, even the two bank notes, and he surrendered to it. Raising his head to the sky, he found himself awed by the dazzling brilliance of the stars at this hour just before sunrise.

FIVE

They stared at him incredulously, then everyone in the café rose at once to meet him. Led by the proprietor and his waiter, uttering a variety of colorful expressions of welcome, they formed a circle around him, embraced him, kissing him on the cheeks. Said Mahran shook hands with each of them, saying politely, "Thanks, Mr. Tarzan. Thanks, friends."

"When was it?"

"Day before yesterday."

"There was supposed to be an amnesty. We were keeping our fingers crossed."

"Thank God I'm out."

"And the rest of the boys?"

"They're all well; their turn will come."

They excitedly exchanged news for a while, until Tarzan, the proprietor, led Said to his own sofa, asking the other men to go back to their places, and the café was quiet again. Nothing had changed. Said felt he'd left it only yesterday. The round room with its brass fittings, the wooden chairs with their straw seats, were just the way they used to be. A handful of customers, some of whom he recognized, sat sipping tea and making deals. Through the open door and out the big window opposite you could see the wasteland stretching into the distance, its thick darkness unrelieved by a single glimmer of light. Its impressive silence broken only by occasional laughter borne in on the dry and refreshing breeze—forceful and clean, like the desert itself—that blew between the window and the door.

Said took the glass of tea from the waiter, raised it to his lips without waiting for it to cool, then turned to the proprietor. "How's business these days?"

Tarzan curled his lower lip. "There aren't many men you can rely on nowadays," he said contemptuously.

"What do you mean? That's too bad."

"They're all lazy, like bureaucrats!"

Said grunted sympathetically "At least a lazy man is better than a traitor. It was thanks to a traitor I had to go to jail, Mr. Tarzan."

"Really? You don't say!"

Said stared at him surprised. "Didn't you hear the story, then?" When Tarzan shook his head sympathetically, Said whispered in his ear, "I need a good revolver."

"If there's anything you need, I'm at your service."

Said patted him on the shoulder gratefully, then began to ask, with some embarrassment, "But I haven't—"

Tarzan interrupted, placing a thick finger on Said's lips, and said, "You don't need to apologize ever to anyone!"

Said savored the rest of his tea, then walked to the

window and stood there, a strong, slim, straight-backed figure of medium height, and let the breeze belly out his jacket, gazing into the pitch-dark wasteland that stretched away ahead of him. The stars overhead looked like grains of sand; and the café felt like an island in the midst of an ocean, or an airplane alone in the sky. Behind him, at the foot of the small hill on which the café stood, lighted cigarettes moved like nearer stars in the hands of those who sat there in the dark seeking fresh air. On the horizon to the west, the lights of Abbasiyya seemed very far away, their distance making one understand how deeply in the desert this café had been placed.

As Said stared out the window, he became aware of the voices of the men who sat outside, sprawled around the hill, enjoying the desert breeze—the waiter was going down to them now, carrying a water pipe with glowing coals, from which sparks flew upward with a crackling noise—their lively conversations punctuated by bursts of laughter. He heard the voice of one young man, obviously enjoying a discussion, say, "Show me a single place on earth where there's any security."

Another one disagreed. "Here where we're sitting, for instance. Aren't we enjoying peace and security now?"

"You see, you say 'now.' There's the calamity."

"But why do we curse our anxiety and fears? In the end don't they save us the trouble of thinking about the future?"

"So you're an enemy of peace and tranquillity."

"When all you have to think about is the hangman's rope around your neck, it's natural enough to fear tranquillity."

"Well, that's a private matter—you can settle it between yourself and the hangman."

"You're chattering away happily because here you're protected by the desert and the dark. But you'll have to go back to the city sometime soon. So what's the use?"

"The real tragedy is that our enemy is at the same time our friend."

"On the contrary, it's that our friend is also our enemy."

"No. It's that we're cowards. Why don't we admit it?"

"Maybe we are cowards. But how can you be brave in this age?"

"Courage is courage."

"And death is death."

"And darkness and the desert are all these things."

What a conversation! What did they mean? Somehow they're giving expression to my own situation, in a manner as shapeless and strange as the mysteries of that night. There was a time when I had youth, energy, and conviction too—the time when I got arms for the national cause and not for the sake of murder. On the other side of this very hill, young men, shabby, but pure in heart, used to train for battle. And their leader was the present inhabitant of villa number 18.

Training himself, training others, spelling out words of wisdom. "Said Mahran," he used to say to me, "a revolver is more important than a loaf of bread. It's more important than the Sufi sessions you keep rushing off to the way your father did." One evening he asked me, "What does a man need in this country, Said?" and without waiting for an answer he said, "He needs a gun and a book: the gun will take care of the past, the book is for the future. Therefore you must train and read." I can still recall his face that night in the students' hostel, his guffaws of laughter, his words: "So you have stolen. You've actually dared to steal. Bravo! Using theft to relieve the exploiters of some of their guilt is absolutely legitimate, Said. Don't ever doubt it."

This open wasteland had borne witness to Said's own skill. Didn't it used to be said that he was Death Incarnate, that his shot never missed? He closed his eyes, relaxing, enjoying the fresh air, until suddenly he felt a hand on his shoulder. And looking around, he saw Tarzan, holding out to him a revolver in his other hand.

"May it be fire for your enemy, God willing," Tarzan said to him.

Said took it. "How much is it, Mr. Tarzan?" he said, inspecting the bolt action.

"It's a present from me"

"No, thank you, I can't accept that. All I ask is that you give me some time until I can afford to pay you."

"How many bullets do you need?"

They walked back to Tarzan's sofa. As they passed

the open doorway, they heard a woman's laughter ringing outside. Tarzan chuckled. "It's Nur, remember her?"

Said looked into the darkness, but could see nothing. "Does she still come here?" he asked.

"Sometimes. She'll be pleased to see you."

"Has she caught anybody?"

"Of course. This time it's the son of the owner of a candy factory." They sat down and Tarzan called the waiter over. "Tell Nur—tactfully—to come here."

It would be nice to see her, to see what time had done to her. She'd hoped to gain his love, but failed. What love he'd had had been the exclusive property of that other, unfaithful woman. He'd been made of stone. There's nothing more heartbreaking than loving someone like that. It had been like a nightingale singing to a rock, a breeze caressing sharp-pointed spikes. Even the presents she'd given he used to give away—to Nabawiyya or Ilish. He patted the gun in his pocket and clenched his teeth.

Nur appeared at the entrance. Unprepared, she stopped in amazement as soon as she saw Said, remaining a few steps away from him. He smiled at her, but looked closely. She'd grown thinner, her face was disguised by heavy makeup, and she was wearing a sexy frock that not only showed her arms and legs but was fitted so tightly to her body that it might have been stretched rubber. What it advertised was that she'd given up all claims to self-respect. So did her bobbed hair, ruffled by the breeze. She ran to him.

"Thank God you're safe," she said, as their hands met, giggling a little to hide her emotion, squeezing him and Tarzan.

"How are you, Nur?" he asked.

"As you can see," Tarzan said for her with a smile, "she's all light, like her name."

"I'm fine," she said. "And you? You look very healthy. But what's wrong with your eyes? They remind me of how you used to look when you were angry."

"What do you mean?" he said with a grin.

"I don't know, it's hard to describe. Your eyes turn a sort of red and your lips start twitching!"

Said laughed. Then, with a touch of sadness, he said, "I suppose your friend will be coming soon to take you back?"

"Oh, he's dead drunk," she said, shaking her head, tossing the hair from her eyes.

"In any case, you're tied to him."

"Would you like me," she said with a sly smile, "to bury him in the sand?"

"No, not tonight. We'll meet again later. I'm told he's a real catch," he added, with a look of interest that did not escape her.

"He sure is. We'll go in his car to the Martyr's Tomb. He likes open spaces."

So he likes open spaces. Over near the Martyr's Tomb.

Her eyelashes fluttered, showing a pretty confusion that increased as her gaze met his. "You see," she said with a pout, "you never think of me."

"It's not true," he said. "You're very dear to me."

"You're only thinking about that poor fish."

Said smiled. "He forms a part of my thinking of you."

"I'll be ruined if they find out," she said with sudden seriousness. "His father's an influential man and he comes from a powerful family. Do you need money?"

"What I really need is a car," he said, standing up. "Try to be completely natural with him," he went on, gently pinching one of her cheeks. "Nothing will happen to frighten you and no one will suspect you. I'm not a kid. When this is done we'll see a lot more of each other than you ever thought possible."

SIX

He knew this stretch of ground. Avoiding the road next to the barracks, he set out across the desert to reach the Martyr's Tomb in the shortest time possible, heading for it as if he had a compass built into his head. As soon as he saw the tomb's big dome in the starlight he began looking for the spot where the car would be tucked away. Walking around the tomb, he scanned the ground as sharply as he could, but it was only when he reached its southern wall that the shape at a little distance became visible. He made for it without another thought, keeping his head low, crouching as he came closer to the car, until he could hear through the silence the sounds of love being made in whispers. *There'll be terror, now, he told himself, in the middle of pleasure, and joy will suddenly vanish, but it's no fault of yours: chaos and confusion envelop us all like the vault of the sky. Didn't Rauf Ilwan used to say that our intentions were good but we lacked order or discipline?*

The breathing inside the car had turned to panting. Almost crawling on his hands and knees, Said crept up until he could touch the door handle. He tightened his grip on the handle, and yanked open the door, shouting, "Don't move!"

Two people cried out in shocked surprise and a pair of heads stared at him in terror. He waved the gun and said, "Don't move or I'll shoot. Get out."

"I beg you," said Nur's voice.

Another voice, throaty, as if strained through sand and gravel, said, "What—what is it you want, please?"

"Get out."

Nur threw herself out of the car, clutching her clothes in one hand, followed by the young man, who stumbled as he struggled to insert his feet in his trousers. Said thrust the gun so menacingly close that the young man began to plead. "No. No. Please don't shoot," he said almost tearfully.

"The money," Said growled.

"In my jacket. In the car."

Said shoved Nur back to the car. "You get in."

Groaning with pain, she climbed in. "Please let me go. For God's sake let me go," she stammered.

"Give me the jacket." He snatched it from her, removed the wallet, and threw the jacket in the man's face. "You have exactly one minute to save your skin." While the young man bolted off in the dark like a comet, Said flung himself into the driver's seat and switched on the engine. The car shot forward with a roar.

"I was really scared," Nur said as she dressed, "as if I hadn't really been expecting you."

"Let's have a drink," he said as soon as they

reached the road, still hurtling forward. She handed him a bottle and he took a swig. He handed it back to her and she did the same.

"Poor man, his knees were shaking," she said.

"You're very kindhearted. As for me, I don't particularly like factory owners."

"You don't like anybody, that's a fact," she said, sitting up and looking ahead. Said didn't feel like trying to charm her and said nothing.

"They'll see me with you!" she squealed when she saw that the car was approaching Abbasiyya. The same thought had occurred to him, so he turned off into a side street that led toward Darrasa and drove a little slower.

"I went to Tarzan's café to get a gun and try to arrange something with an old friend, a taxi driver. But now look how luck has sent me this car!"

"Don't you think I'm always useful?"

"Always. And you were fantastic, too. Why don't you go on the stage?"

"In the beginning I was really scared."

"But later?"

"I hope I was convincing, so he won't suspect me."

"He was so out of his mind with fear he wasn't capable of suspecting anything."

"Why do you need a gun and a car?" she asked, putting her head close to his.

"They're the tools of the trade."

"Heaven! When did you get out of jail?"

"The day before yesterday."

"And you're already thinking of doing that again?"

"Have you ever found it easy to change your job?"

Staring ahead at the dark road, visible only in the car's headlights, Nur made no reply. At the turn, the hill of the Muqattam loomed nearer, like a chunk of the night more solid than the rest.

"Do you realize how sad I was," she said softly, "when I heard you'd been sent up?"

"No. How sad?"

"When will you stop being sarcastic?" She sounded a little annoyed.

"But I'm dead serious. And absolutely certain of the sincerity of your affection."

"You have no heart."

"They've got it locked up in prison, according to regulations!"

"You were heartless long before you ever went to jail."

Why does she harp on the subject of affection? She should talk to that treacherous woman, and the dogs, and the little girl who rejected me. "One day we'll succeed in finding it," he said.

"Where will you stay tonight? Does your wife know where you are?"

"I don't think so."

"Are you going home, then?"

"I don't think so. Not tonight, in any case."

"Come to my place."

"Do you live alone?"

"Yes, in Sharia Najm al-Din beyond the cemetery at Bab el-Nasr."

"Number?"

"There's only one house on the street; it's over a sackcloth store and right behind it is the cemetery."

"What a great location!" Said laughed.

Nur laughed, too. "No one knows me there and no one's ever visited me. You'll find it on the top floor." She waited for his reply, but he was busy watching the road, which began to narrow between the hill and the houses that came after Sheikh Ali al-Junaydi's place. At the top of Sharia Darrasa he stopped the car and turned toward her.

"This is a good place for you to get out."

"Won't you come with me?"

"I'll come to you later on."

"But where are you going at this hour of night?"

"You go straight to the police station now. Tell them exactly what happened as if you had nothing to do with me and give them a description of a person completely different from me. Say he's fat, fair-skinned, and has an old scar on his right cheek. Tell them I kidnapped you, robbed you, and raped you.

"Raped me?"

"In the desert at Zinhum," he went on, ignoring her exclamation, "and say I threw you out of the car and drove away."

"Are you really coming to see me?"

"Yes, that's a solemn promise. Will you be able to act as well in the police station as you did in the car?"

"I hope so."

"Goodbye, then." And he drove away.

SEVEN

To kill them both—Nabawiyya and Ilish—at the same time would be a triumph. Even better would be to settle with Rauf Ilwan, too, then escape, go abroad if possible. But who'll look after Sana? The thorn in my side. You always act impulsively, Said, without thinking, but you mustn't rush this time; you must wait until you've arranged things, then swoop like an eagle. But there's no point in delay either: you're a hunted man—you became a hunted man as soon as they knew you were coming out—and now, after the car incident, the search will be intensified. Only a few pounds in the wallet of the factory owner's son—another stroke of bad luck. If you don't strike soon everything will collapse. Who'll look after Sana, though? That thorn again. She rejected me but I still love her. Should I spare your unfaithful mother for your sake, then? I must find the answer right away.

He was hovering on foot in the pitch-darkness surrounding the house at the crossroads where two lanes met in Imam Way. The car was parked at the top of the road, back toward the Citadel square. Shops were closed, the road was deserted, and no one seemed to be looking for him: at such an hour every creature took shelter, blind and unsuspecting, in his hole. Said could easily have taken further precautions, but he was not going to be diverted from his purpose, even if it meant Sana's having to live alone all her life. For treachery, Mr. Rauf, is an abomination.

He looked up at the windows of the house, his hand clutching the revolver in his pocket. Treachery is abominable, Ilish, and for the living to enjoy life it is imperative that criminal and vicious elements be eradicated. Keeping close to the wall, he approached the door, then entered the house and cautiously climbed the pitch-dark stairs, passing the first floor, then the second to the third. Right. And there was the flat, the door, snugly closed on the most rotten intentions and desires. If he knocked, who would answer? Would it be Nabawiyya? Was the police detective perhaps lurking somewhere? There was hellfire for them both even if he had to break into the flat. He must act at once. It was not right that Ilish Sidra should stay alive for even one day while Said Mahran was a free man. *You'll get away without a scratch, just as easily as you have scores of times: you can scale an apartment building in seconds, jump unhurt from a third-floor window —even fly if you wish!*

It seems you must knock on the door. But knocking might arouse suspicion, especially at this hour. Nabawiyya would fill the world with her screams, and bring some cowardly fools. That detective, too. So you'd better break the little glass pane in the door.

He'd had the idea in the car on the way here and now he came back to it. He drew his gun and gave the glass one blow through the twisted bars that protected it. As the glass broke and the pieces scattered, it made a noise like a choked-off scream in the silent night. He flattened himself against the wall, next to the door and waited, his heart beating fast and his eyes peering into the darkness of the entrance hall, where the gun was pointed. A man's voice, which he could recognize as Ilish Sidra's despite the throbbing noise in his temples, said, "Who's there?" and a door to the left opened, giving a faint light by which he could just make out the figure of a man approaching cautiously. Said pressed the trigger and the gun roared like a demon in the night. The man cried out and began to fall, but another bullet struck him even before he hit the floor, where he lay like a sack. A woman shrieked for help—Nabawiyya's voice. "Your turn will come! There's no escape from me! I'm the devil himself!" he shouted as he turned to escape, leaping down the stairs so recklessly that he reached the bottom in seconds, where he paused briefly to listen, then slipped out. Once outside he walked away calmly, keeping close to the wall, leaving behind him the sounds of windows opening and voices questioning and vague cries whose words he could not make out. When he reached the place at the top of the road where he'd parked the car, and had pulled open the door to get in, he spotted a policeman running from the square toward Imam Way. Ducking down, he hid on the floor of the car as the policeman ran on past toward the screaming, remaining still until the footsteps sounded far enough away, then he sat up behind the steering wheel and sped off. At the square he slowed down to a normal speed, the din still haunting his senses and settling at last within his nerves. He felt stunned. Confusion pervaded his whole being and he was only half aware of what he did as he drove on. *A murderer! But there's still Rauf Ilwan, the high-class traitor, really much more important and dangerous than Ilish Sidra. A murderer! You are now one of those who commit murder; you have a new identity now and a new destiny! You used to take precious goods—now you take worthless lives!*

Your turn will come, Nabawiyya. There's no escape from me. I'm the devil himself. I've granted you life, thanks to Sana, but I've enclosed you in a punishment greater than death; fear of death, the unrelenting terror. As long as I live you'll never enjoy the taste of peace.

He came down Sharia Muhammad Ali in a stupor, without a thought to where he was going. Many people would now have a murderer on their minds. The murderer must hide. He must take care to avoid the rope and the gallows. *You must never have the executioner asking what your last wish is, Said! Oh no. The government must be made to ask you this question, but on some better occasion!*

When he returned to full awareness he found he'd covered the last stretch of Sharia al-Gaysh and was speeding toward Abbasiyya. Alarmed to find himself unexpectedly returning to a place of danger, he doubled his speed and in a few minutes reached Manshiyyat al-Bakri, where he stopped at the first street branching from the main road, quietly abandoned the car, and walked away without looking left or right, slowly, as if exercising his legs. He felt numbness, then some sort of pain, as if in reaction to the great nervous effort he had made. *Nowhere is safe for you now. Or ever after. And Nur? It would be risky to go to her place tonight, of all nights, what with the investigations and suspicions that are bound to ensue. Darkness must extend from now on to all eternity.*

EIGHT

He pushed the Sheikh's door, met no resistance, entered, closed it behind him, and found himself in the open courtyard where the palm tree towered, as if stretched upward into space as high as the watchful stars. What a superb place for hiding, he thought. The Sheikh's room was open at night, just as it was by day. There it stood, pitch-black, as if waiting for his return, and he walked toward it quietly. He heard the voice muttering but could only distinguish the word "Allah," "God!" It went on muttering as if the Sheikh were unaware or perhaps reluctant to acknowledge his presence.

Said withdrew into a corner at the left of the room close to his pile of books and flung himself down on the rush mat, still in his suit and shoes and carrying his revolver. He stretched out his legs, supporting his trunk on the palms of his hands, his head falling back in exhaustion. His head felt like a beehive, but there was nothing he could do.

You wish to recall the sound of the bullet and the screams of Nabawiyya, feeling happy again that you did not hear Sana scream. You'd better greet the Sheikh, but your voice is too weak to say "Peace be upon you!" There's this feeling of helplessness, as if you were drowning. And you thought you were going to sleep like a log as soon as your skin touched the floor!

How the righteous and God-fearing would have shuddered, turned away from him in fright—until recitation of the name of God had made them less particular, less hard of heart. When would this strange man go to sleep? But the strange old man now raised his voice and began to sing: "In my view, passion is nothing but ingratitude unless it issues from my witnesses." And in a voice that seemed to fill the room, he said, "The eyes of their hearts are open, but those in their heads are closed!" Said smiled in spite of himself. So that's why he is not aware of my presence. But then I, too, am not fully aware of my own self.

The call to the dawn prayers rose above the quiet waves of the night. It reminded him of a night he'd once spent sleepless until the same call to the dawn prayers, excited over some special joy promised for the following day. On that occasion, he'd got up as soon as he heard the call, happy at release from a night of torment, had looked out of the window at the blue dawn and the smiling sunrise, and had rubbed his hands in anticipation of whatever it was he'd been about to enjoy, something he had since completely forgotten. And therefore he loved the dawn, which he associated with the singing of the prayer call, the deep blue sky, the smile of the approaching sunrise, and that unremembered joy.

It was dawn now, but his exhaustion was so great he could not move, not even to shift his revolver. The

Sheikh rose to perform his prayers. Showing no awareness of Said's presence, he lit the oil lamp, spread out the prayer mat, took up his position on it, then suddenly asked, "Aren't you going to perform the dawn prayers?"

Said was so tired he was incapable of giving an answer, and no sooner had the Sheikh begun his prayers than he dropped off to sleep.

He dreamt that he was in jail, being whipped despite his good conduct, screaming shamelessly, but not offering any resistance. They gave him milk to drink. Suddenly he saw little Sana lashing Rauf Ilwan with a whip at the bottom of a staircase. He heard the sound of a Koranic recitation and had the impression that someone had died, but then he found himself, a wanted man, somehow involved in a car chase! The car he was driving was incapable of speed—there was something wrong with its engine—and he had to begin shooting in every direction. Suddenly, Rauf Ilwan appeared from the radio in the dashboard, grabbed his wrist before Said was able to kill him, and tightened his grip so mercilessly that he was able to snatch the revolver. At this point Said Mahran said to him, "Kill me if you wish, but my daughter is innocent. It wasn't she who whipped you at the bottom of the staircase. It was her mother, Nabawiyya, at the instigation of Ilish Sidra." Escaping his pursuers, Said then slipped into the circle of Sufi chanters gathered around Sheikh al-Junaydi, but the Sheikh denied him. "Who are you?" he asked. "How did you come to be with us?"

He told him he was Said Mahran, son of Amm Mahran, his old disciple, and reminded him of the old days, but the Sheikh demanded his identity card. Said was surprised and objected that a Sufi disciple didn't need an identity card, that in the eyes of the mystical order the righteous and the sinner were alike. When the Sheikh replied that he did not like the righteous and wanted to see Said's identity card to make sure that Said was really a sinner, Said handed him the revolver, explaining that every missing bullet meant a murder, but the Sheikh insisted on seeing his card; the government instructions, he said, were stringent on this point. Said was astounded: why did the government interfere with the affairs of the order? he asked. The Sheikh informed him that it had all resulted from a suggestion by their great authority Rauf Ilwan, who had been nominated for the post of Supreme Sheikh. Stunned with amazement for the third time, Said protested that Rauf was nothing but a traitor who had only criminal thoughts, and the Sheikh retorted that that was why he'd been recommended for this responsible position. He added that Rauf had promised to offer a new exegesis of the Holy Koran, giving all possible interpretations, so as to benefit each man according to his purchasing power; the money this beneficent move would bring in would be invested in setting up clubs for shooting, hunting, and committing suicide. Said declared that he was prepared to act as treasurer for the new Exegesis Administration and that Rauf Ilwan would no doubt testify to his integrity as one of his brightest former pupils. At that point the Sheikh intoned the opening chapter of the Koran, lanterns were suspended from the trunk of the palm tree, and a reciter chanted, "Blessed be ye, O people of Egypt, our lord Husayn is now yours."

When he opened his eyes the whole world looked red, empty and meaningless. The Sheikh sat in repose, everything about him, from his loose garment to his skullcap and beard, a shiny white, and at Said's first movement the Sheikh turned his gaze on him. Said sat up hurriedly and looked apologetic, assailed by memories that rushed into his mind like roaring flames.

"It is now late afternoon," said the Sheikh, "and you haven't had a bite of food."

Said looked first at the hole in the wall, then at the Sheikh, and muttered absentmindedly, "Late afternoon!"

"Yes. I thought to myself: Let him sleep. God presents His gifts as His will alone decides."

Said was suddenly troubled. He wondered if anybody had seen him asleep there all day. "I was aware of many people coming in while I was asleep," he lied.

"You were aware of nothing. But one man brought me my lunch, another came to sweep the place, water the cactus, tend the palm tree, and get the courtyard ready for God's loving worshippers."

"What time are they coming?" he said, a little worried.

"At sunset. When did you arrive?"

"At dawn."

The Sheikh sat silent for a while, stroking his beard, then said, "You are very wretched, my son!"

"Why?" said Said, anxious to know the answer.

"You've had a long sleep, but you know no rest. Just like a child laid under the fire of the blazing sun. Your burning heart yearns for shade, yet continues forward under the fire of the sun. Haven't you learned to walk yet?"

Said rubbed his bloodshot almond-shaped eyes. "It's a disturbing thought, to be seen asleep by others."

"The world is unaware of him who is unaware of it," the Sheikh replied, showing no concern.

Said's hand passed lightly over the pocket where he kept the revolver. He wondered what the Sheikh would do if he were to point his gun at him. Would his maddening composure be shaken?

"Are you hungry?" the Sheikh asked.

"No."

"If it is true that man can be poor in God, so is it true man can be rich in Him," the Sheikh went on, his eyes almost smiling.

If, that is, the first proposition is indeed true! thought Said. "Well then, Master," he said lightly, "what would you have done if you'd been afflicted with a wife like mine and if your daughter had rejected you as mine has me?"

A look of pity appeared in the old man's clear eyes. "God's slave is owned by God alone!"

Cut off your tongue before it betrays you and confesses your crime! You wish to tell him everything. He probably doesn't need to be told. He may even have seen you fire the gun. And he may be able to see much more than that.

A voice outside the window hawked *The Sphinx*. Said got up at once, walked to the window, called the newspaper boy, handed him a small coin, and returned with the paper to where he'd been sitting, forgetting all about the Sheikh, his eyes riveted to a huge black headline: "Dastardly Murder in the Citadel Quarter!" He devoured the lines beneath in a flash, not understanding anything. Was this another murder? His own picture was there and so were pictures of Nabawiyya and Ilish Sidra, but who was that bloodstained man? His own life story was staring at him, too, sensational doings blown in every direction like dust in a whirlwind—the story of a man who came out of prison to find his wife married to one of his underlings. But who was the bloodstained man? How had his bullet entered this stranger's chest? This victim was someone else, and Said was seeing him for the first time in his life. *You'd better start reading again.*

The same day he'd visited them with the detective and Ilish's friends, Ilish Sidra and Nabawiyya had moved out of their flat and another family had moved in, so the voice he'd heard had not been Ilish Sidra's nor had the screams been Nabawiyya's. The body was that of one Shaban Husayn, the new tenant, who'd worked in a haberdashery in Sharia Muhammad Ali. Said Mahran had come to murder his wife and his old friend, but had killed the new tenant instead. A neighbor testified that he'd seen Said Mahran leaving the house after the murder and that he'd shouted for the police but his voice had been lost in the din that had filled the entire street.

A failure. It was insane. And pointless. The rope would be after him now, while Ilish sat safe and secure. The truth was as clear as the bottom of an open tomb.

He tore his eyes away from the paper and found the Sheikh staring through the window at the sky, smiling. The smile, for some reason or other, frightened Said: he wished he could stand at the window and look at exactly the same bit of sky the Sheikh was looking at so he could see what it was that made him smile. But the wish was unfulfilled.

Let the Sheikh smile and keep his secret, he thought. Before long the disciples would be here and some of them who'd seen the picture in the paper might recognize him; thousands and thousands would be gaping at his picture now, in a mixture of terror and titillation. Said's life was finished, spent to no purpose; he was a hunted man and would be to the end of his days; he was alone, and would have to beware of even his own reflection in a mirror—alive but without real life. Like a mummy. He'd have to flee like a rat from one hole to another, threatened by poison, cats, and the clubs of disgusted human beings, suffering all this while his enemies kicked up their heels.

The Sheikh turned to him, saying gently, "You are tired. Go and wash your face."

"Yes," Said said irritably, folding up the paper. "I'll go—and relieve you of the sight of my face."

With even greater gentleness, the Sheikh said, "This is your home."

"True, but why shouldn't I have another place of shelter?"

The Sheikh bowed his head, replying, "If you had another you would never have come to me."

You must go up the hill and stay there until dark. Avoid the light. Shelter in the dark. Hell, it's all a waste of time. You've killed Shaban Husayn. I wonder who you are, Shaban. We never knew each other. Did you have children? Did you ever imagine that one day you would be killed for no reason—that you'd be killed because Nabawiyya Sulayman married Ilish Sidra? That you'd be killed in error but Ilish, Nabawiyya, and Rauf would not be killed in justice? I, the murderer, understand nothing. Not even Sheikh Ali al-Junaydi himself can understand anything. I've tried to solve part of the riddle, but have only succeeded in unearthing an even greater one. He sighed aloud.

"How tired you are," said the Sheikh.

"And it is your world that makes me tired!"

"That is what we sing of sometimes," the Sheikh said placidly.

Said rose, then said, as he was about to go, "Farewell, my Master."

"Utterly meaningless words, whatever you intend by them," the Sheikh remonstrated. "Say rather: until we meet again."

NINE

God, it's dark! I'd be better off like a bat. Why is that smell of hot fat seeping out from under some door at this hour of the night? When will Nur be back? Will she come alone? And can I stay in her flat long enough to be forgotten? You might perhaps be thinking you've got rid of me forever now, Rauf? But with this revolver, if I have any luck, I can do wonderful things. With this revolver I can awake those who are asleep. They're the root of the trouble. They're the ones who've made creatures like Nabawiyya, Ilish, and Rauf Ilwan possible.

There was a sound like footsteps climbing the stairs. When he was sure he heard someone coming, he crouched and looked down through the banisters. A faint light was moving slowly along the wall. The light of a match, he thought. The footsteps came higher, heavy and slow. To let her know he was there and to avoid surprising her, he cleared his throat with a loud rasp.

"Who is it?" she said apprehensively.

Said leaned his head out between the banisters as far as he could and replied in a whisper, "Said Mahran."

She ran the rest of the way up and stopped in front of him out of breath. The match was almost out.

"It's you!" she said, breathless and happy, seizing his arm. "I'm sorry. Have you been waiting long?"

Opening the door to the flat, she led him in by the arm, switched on the light in a bare rectangular hall, then drew him into a reception room, square and somewhat larger, where she rushed to the window and flung it open wide to release the stifling air.

"It was midnight when I got here," he said, flinging himself down on one of two sofas that stood face to face. "I've waited for ages."

"She sat down opposite him, moving a pile of scraps of cloth and dress cuttings. "You know what?" she said. "I'd given up hope. I didn't think you'd really come."

Their tired eyes met. "Even after my definite promise?" he said, hiding his frozen feelings with a smile.

She smiled back faintly, without answering. Then she said, "Yesterday they kept questioning me at the police station over and over. They nearly killed me. Where's the car?"

"I thought I'd better dump it somewhere, even though I need it." He took off his jacket and tossed it on the sofa next to him. His brown shirt was caked with sweat and dust. "They'll find it and give it back to its owner, as you'd expect of a government that favors some thieves more than others."

"What did you do with it yesterday?"

"Nothing whatever, in fact. Anyway, you'll know everything at the proper time." He gazed at the open window, took a deep breath, and said, "It must face north. Really fresh air."

"It's open country from here to Bab al-Noor. All around here is the cemetery."

"That's why the air isn't polluted," he said with a grin. *She's looking at you as if she could eat you up, but you only feel bored, annoyed. Why can't you stop brooding over your wounded pride and enjoy her?*

"I'm terribly sorry you had to wait so long on the landing."

"Well, I'm going to be your guest for quite some time," he said, giving her a strange, scrutinizing look.

She lifted her head, raised her chin, and said happily, "Stay here all your life, if you like."

"Until I move over to the neighbors'!" he said with another grin, pointing through the window. She seemed preoccupied. She didn't seem to hear his joke. "Won't your people ask about you?" she said.

"I have no people," he replied, looking down at his gym shoes.

"I mean your wife."

She means pain and fury and wasted bullets! What she wants is to hear a humiliating confession; she'll only find that a locked heart becomes increasingly difficult to unlock. But what is the point of lying when the newspapers are screaming with sensation?

"I said I have no people." Now you're wondering what my words mean. Your face is beaming with happiness. But I hate this joy. And I can see now that your face has lost whatever bloom it had, particularly under the eyes.

"Divorced?" she asked.

"Yes. When I was in jail. But let's close the subject," he said, waving his hand impatiently.

"The bitch!" she said angrily. "A man like you deserves to be waited for, even if he's been sent up for life!"

How sly she is! But a man like me doesn't like to be pitied. Beware of sympathy! "The truth is that I neglected her far too much." What a waste for bullets to strike the innocent!

"Anyway, she isn't the kind of woman who deserves you."

True. Neither is any other woman. But Nabawiyya's still full of vitality, while you're hovering on the brink: one puff of wind would be enough to blow you out. You only arouse pity in me. "No one must know I am here."

Laughing, as if sure she possessed him forever, she said, "Don't worry; I'll keep you hidden all right." Then, hopefully, she added, "But you haven't done anything really serious, have you?"

He dismissed the question by shrugging nonchalantly.

She stood up and said, "I'll get some food for you. I do have food and drink. Do you remember how cold you used to be to me?"

"I had no time for love then."

She eyed him reproachfully. "Is anything more important than love? I often wondered if your heart wasn't made of stone. When you went to jail, no one grieved as much as I did."

"That's why I came to you instead of anybody else."

"But you only ran into me by chance," she said with a pout. "You might even have forgotten all about me!"

"Do you think I can't find anywhere else?" he said, framing his face into a scowl.

As if to head off an outburst, she came up close to him and took his cheeks between the palms of her hands. "The guards at the zoo won't let visitors tease the lion. I'd forgotten that. Please forgive me. But your face is burning and your beard is bristly. Why not have a cold shower?" His smile showed her he welcomed the idea. "Off you go to the bathroom, then! When you come out you'll find some food ready. We'll eat in the bedroom, it's much nicer than this room. It looks out over the cemetery, too."

TEN

What a lot of graves there are, laid out as far as the eye can see. Their headstones are like hands raised in surrender, though they are beyond being threatened by anything. A city of silence and truth, where success and failure, murderer and victim, come together, where thieves and policemen lie side by side in peace for the first and last time.

Nur's snoring seemed likely to end only when she awoke in late afternoon.

You'll stay in this prison until the police forget you. And will they ever really forget? The graves remind you that death cheats the living. They speak of betrayal; and thus they make you remember Nabawiyya, Ilish, and Rauf, telling you that you yourself are dead, ever since that unseeing bullet was fired.

But you still have bullets of fire.

At the sound of Nur's yawning, loud, like a groan, he turned away from the window shutters toward the bed. Nur was sitting up, naked, her hair disheveled, looking unrested and run-down. But she smiled as she said, "I dreamed you were far away and I was going out of my mind waiting for you."

"That was a dream," he observed grimly. "In fact,

you're the one who's going out and I'm the one who'll wait."

She went into the bathroom, emerged again drying her hair; and he followed her hands as they re-created her face in a new form, happy and young. She was, like himself, thirty years old, but she lied outright, hoping to appear younger, adding to the multitude of sins and sillinesses which are openly committed. But theft, unfortunately, was not one of them.

"Don't forget the papers," he reminded her at the door.

When she'd gone he moved into the reception room and flung himself down on one of the sofas. Now he was alone in the full sense of the word, without even his books, which he'd left with Sheikh Ali. He stared up at the cracked white ceiling, a dull echo of the threadbare carpet, killing time. The setting sun flashed through the open window, like a jewel being carried by a flight of doves from one point in time to the next.

Your coldness, Sana, was very disquieting. Like seeing these graves. I don't know if we'll meet again, or where or when. You'll certainly never love me now. Not in this life, so full of badly aimed bullets, desires gone astray. What's left behind is a dangling chain of regrets. The first link was the students' hostel on the road to Giza. Ilish didn't matter much, but Nabawiyya—she'd shaken him, torn him up by the roots. If only a deceit could be as plainly read in the face as fever or an infectious disease! Then beauty would never be false and many a man would be spared the ravages of deception.

That grocery near the students' hostel, where Nabawiyya used to come shopping, gripping her bowl. She was always so nicely dressed, much neater than the other servant girls, which was why she'd been known as the "Turkish lady's maid." The rich, proud old Turkish woman, who lived alone at the end of the road, in a house at the center of a big garden, insisted that everyone who worked for her should be good-looking, clean, and well dressed. So Nabawiyya always appeared with her hair neatly combed and plaited in a long pigtail, and wearing slippers. Her peasant's gown flowed around a sprightly and nimble body, and even those not bewitched by her agreed that she was a fine example of country beauty with her dark complexion, her round, full face, her brown eyes, her small chubby nose, and her lips moist with the juices of life. There was a small green tattoo mark on her chin like a beauty spot.

You used to stand at the entrance to the students' hostel and wait for her after work, staring up the street until her fine form with her adorable gait appeared in the distance. As she stepped closer and closer, you'd glow with anticipation. She was like some lovely melody, welcomed wherever she went. As she slipped in among the dozens of women standing at the grocer's, your eyes would follow her, drunk with ecstasy. She'd disappear and emerge again, your desire and curiosity increasing all the time—so did your impulse to do something, no matter what, by word, gesture, or invocation—and she'd move off on her way home, to disappear for the rest of the day and another whole night. And you'd let out a long, bitter sigh and your elation would subside; the birds in the roadside trees would cease their song and a cold autumn breeze would suddenly spring up from nowhere.

But then you notice that her form is reacting to your stare, that she's swaying coquettishly as she walks, and you stand there no longer, but, with your natural impetuosity, hurry after her along the road. Then at the lone palm tree at the edge of the fields you bar her way. She's dumbfounded by your audacity, or pretends to be, and asks you indignantly who you might be. You reply in feigned surprise, "Who might I be? You really ask who I am? Don't you know? I'm known to every inch of your being!"

"I don't like ill-mannered people!" she snaps.

"Neither do I. I'm like you, I hate ill-mannered people. Oh no. On the contrary, I admire good manners, beauty, and gentleness. And all of those things are you! You still don't know who I am? I must carry that basket for you and see you to the door of your house."

"I don't need your help," she says, "and don't ever stand in my way again!" With that she walks away, but with you at her side, encouraged by the faint smile slipping through her pretense of indignation, which you receive like the first cool breeze on a hot and sultry night. Then she had said, "Go back; you must! My mistress sits at the window and if you come one step more she'll see you."

"But I'm a very determined fellow," you reply, "and if you want me to go back, you'll have to come along with me. Just a few steps. Back to the palm tree. You see, I've got to

talk to you. And why shouldn't I? Am I not respectable enough?"

She shakes her head vigorously, but, murmuring an angry protest, she does slow down, her neck arched like an angry cat's. She did slow down and I no longer doubt I've won, that Nabawiyya is not indifferent and knows very well how I stand sighing there at the students' hostel. You know that casual stares in the street will become something big in your life, in hers, and in the world at large, too, which would grow larger as a result.

"Till tomorrow, then," you say, stopping there, afraid for her, afraid of the biting tongue of the old Turk who lives like an enigma at the bottom of the street. So you return to the palm tree and climb it, quick as a monkey, out of sheer high spirits, then jump down again, from ten feet up, into a plot of green. Then you go back to the hostel, singing, in your deep voice, like a bull in ecstasy.

And later, when circumstances sent you to al-Zayyat Circus, to work that took you from quarter to quarter, village to village, you feared that "out of sight, out of mind" might well be applied to you and you asked her to marry you. Yes, you asked her to marry you, in the good old legal, traditional Muslim way, standing outside the university that you had —unfairly—been unable to enter, though so many fools did. There was no light in the street or the sky, just a big crescent moon over the horizon. Gazing shyly down at the ground, her forehead reflecting the pale moonlight, she seemed full of happiness. You told her about your good wages, your excellent prospects, and your neat ground-floor flat in Darrasa, on

Jabal Road, near Sheikh Ali's house. "You'll get to know the godly Sheikh," you said, "when we marry. And we've got to have the wedding as soon as possible. After all, our love has lasted quite a while already. You'll have to leave the old lady now."

"I'm an orphan, you know. There's only my aunt at Sidi al-Arbain."

"That's fine."

Then you kissed her under the crescent moon. The wedding was so lovely that everyone talked about it ever after. From Zayyat I got a wedding present of ten pounds. Ilish Sidra seemed absolutely overjoyed at it all, as if it was his own wedding, playing the part of the faithful friend while he was really no friend at all. And the oddest thing of all is that you were taken in by him—you, clever old you, smart enough to scare the devil himself, you the hero and Ilish your willing slave, admiring, flattering, and doing everything to avoid upsetting you, happy to pick up the scraps of your labor, your smartness. You were sure you could have sent him and Nabawiyya off together alone, into the very deserts where our Lord Moses wandered, and that all the time he'd keep seeing you between himself and her and would never step out of line. How could she ever give up a lion and take to a dog? She's rotten to the core, rotten enough to deserve death and damnation. For sightless bullets not to stray, blindly missing their vile and evil targets, and hit innocent people, leaving others torn with remorse and rage and on the verge of insanity. Compelled to forget everything good in life, the way you used to play as a kid in the street, innocent first love, your wedding night, Sana's birth and seeing her little face, hearing her cry, carrying her in your arms for the first time. All the smiles you never counted—how you wish you'd counted them. And how she looked—you wish it was one of the things you've forgotten—when she was frightened, that screaming of hers that shook the ground and made springs and breezes dry up. All the good feelings that ever were.

The shadows are lengthening now. It's getting dark in the room and outside the window. The silence of the graves is more intense, but you can't switch on the light. The flat must look the way it always has when Nur is out. Your eyes will get used to the dark, the way they did to prison and all those ugly faces. And you can't start drinking, either, lest you bump into something or shout out loud. The flat must stay as silent as the grave; even the dead mustn't know you're here. God alone can tell how long you'll have to stay here and how patient in this jail. Just as He alone could tell you'd kill Shaban Husayn and not Ilish Sidra.

Well, you'll have to go out sooner or later, to take a walk in the night, even if only to safe places. But let's postpone that until the police are worn out looking for you. And let's hope to God Shaban Husayn isn't buried in one of these graves here; this run-down quarter could hardly stand the strain of such a painful irony of fate. Just keep cool, keep patient, until Nur comes back. You must not ask when Nur will come back. You'll have to put up with the dark, the silence, and the loneliness—for as long as the world refuses to change its naughty ways. Nur, poor girl, is caught in it, too. What, after all, is her love for you but a bad habit, getting stuck on someone who's already dead of pain and anger, is put off by her affection no less than by her ageing looks, who doesn't really know what to do with her except maybe drink with her, toasting, as it were, defeat and grief, and pity her for her worthy but hopeless efforts. And in the end you can't even forget she's a woman. Like that slinking bitch Nabawiyya, who'll be in mortal fear until the rope's safely installed around your neck or some rotten bullet is lodged in your heart. And the police will tell such lies that you'll be cut off forever from Sana. She'll never even know the truth of your love for her, as if that, too, was just a bullet that went astray.

Sleep came over Said Mahran and he dozed off for a while on the sofa, unaware that he had been dreaming in his sleep until he awoke, to find himself in complete darkness, still alone in Nur's flat in Sharia Najm al-Din, where Ilish Sidra had not surprised him and had not fired a hail of bullets at him. He had no idea what time it was.

Suddenly he heard the rattle of a key in the lock and then the door being closed. A light in the hallway went on and filtered in above the door. Nur came in smiling, carrying a big parcel. She kissed him and said, "Let's have a feast! I've brought home a restaurant, a delicatessen, and a patisserie all in one!"

"You've been drinking," he said as he kissed her.

"I have to; it's part of my job. I'll take a bath, then come back. Here are the papers for you."

His eyes followed her as she left, then he buried himself in the newspapers, both morning and evening. There was nothing that was news to him, but there was clearly enormous interest in both the crime and its perpetrator, far more than he'd expected, especially in *Al-Zahra*, Rauf Ilwan's paper. It discussed at length his history as a burglar and the list of the exploits revealed at his trial, with stories about the great houses of the rich he had burglarized, comments on his character, his latent insanity, and an analysis of "the criminal boldness that finally led to bloodshed."

What enormous black headlines! Thousands upon thousands must be discussing his crimes at that moment, all amused at Nabawiyya's infidelity and laying bets as to what his fate would be. He was the very center of the news, the man of the hour, and the thought filled him with both apprehension and pride, conflicting emotions that were so intense they almost tore him apart. Meanwhile, so many other thoughts and ideas crowded in confusion into his mind that a kind of intoxication seemed to engulf him. He felt sure he was about to do something truly extraordinary, even miraculous; and he wished he could somehow communicate with all the people outside, to tell them what was making him—there all alone in the silence—burst with emotion, to convince them that he'd win in the end, even if only after death.

He was quite alone, separate from everyone else. They didn't even know, did not comprehend the language of silence and solitude. They didn't understand that they themselves were silent and alone sometimes, and that the mirrors dimly reflecting their own images were in fact deceptive, making them falsely imagine they were seeing people unknown to themselves.

His mind's eye focused on the photograph of Sana with a sense of wonder, and he was deeply moved. Then, in his imagination, he conjured up all their pictures—his own wild-looking self, Nabawiyya, looking like a whore—coming back to the picture of Sana. She was smiling. Yes. Smiling. Because she could not see him and because she knew nothing. He scrutinized her intensely, overwhelmed by the sense that he'd failed, that the night out there through the window was sighing in some kind of sympathetic sadness, desperately wishing he could run away with her to some place known to no one else. He yearned to see her, if only as his last wish on earth before his execution.

He went over to the other sofa to pick up the scissors lying on a pile of pieces of fabric, then returned to snip the picture carefully out of the newspaper. By the time Nur emerged from the bathroom he felt calmer. When she called him, he went into the bedroom, wondering how she could have brought him all those news reports and know nothing of them herself.

She'd spent a lot of money. As he sat by her side on a sofa, facing the food-covered table, his mouth watered, and to show his pleasure he stroked her moist hair and murmured, "You know, there aren't many women like you."

She tied a red scarf around her head and began filling the glasses, smiling at the compliment. To see her sitting there, proud and confident of having him, if only for a while, made him feel somehow glad. She was wearing no makeup over her light brown skin and she looked invigorated from her bath, like a dish of good food, somehow, modest and fresh.

"You can say things like that!" she said, giving him a quizzical stare. "Sometimes I almost think the police know more about kindness than you."

"No, do believe me, I'm happy being with you."

"Truly?"

"Yes. Truly. You're so kind, so good. I don't know why anyone could resist you."

"Wasn't I like that in the old days?"

No easy victory can ever make one forget a bloody defeat! "At that time, I just wasn't an affectionate person."

"And now?"

"Let's have a drink and enjoy ourselves," he said, picking up his glass.

They set about the food and drink with gusto, until she said, "How did you spend your time?"

"Between the shadows and the graves," he said, dipping a piece of meat in tahini. "Do you have any family buried here?"

"No, mine are all buried in al-Balyana, God rest their souls."

Only the sounds of their eating and the clink of glasses and dishes on the tray broke the silence, until Said said, "I'm going to ask you to buy some cloth for me—something suitable for an officer's uniform."

"An army officer?"

"You didn't know I learned tailoring in jail?"

"But why do you want it?" she said uneasily.

"Ah, well, the time has come for me to do my military service."

"Don't you understand I don't want to lose you again?"

"Don't worry about me at all," he said with extraordinary confidence. "If no one had given me away the police would never have caught me."

Nur sighed, still troubled.

"You're not in any danger yourself, are you?" Said asked, grinning, his mouth stuffed with food. "No highwayman's going to waylay you in the desert, right?"

They laughed together, and she leaned over and kissed him full on the lips. Their lips were equally sticky.

"The truth is," she said, "that to live at all we've got to be afraid of nothing."

"Not even death?" Said said, nodding toward the window.

"Listen, I even forget that, too, when time brings me together with someone I love."

Astonished at the strength and tenacity of her affection, Said relaxed and let himself feel a mixture of compassion, respect, and gratitude toward Nur.

A moth overhead made love to a naked light bulb in the dead of the night.

ELEVEN

Not a day passes without the graveyard welcoming new guests. Why, it's as though there's nothing more left to do but crouch behind the shutters watching these endless progressions of death. It's the mourners who deserve one's sympathy, of course. They come in one weeping throng and then they go away drying their tears and conversing, as if while they're here some force stronger than death itself has convinced them to stay alive.

That was how your own parents were buried: your father, Amm Mahran, the kindly concierge of the student's hostel, who died middle-aged after a hard but honest and satisfying life. You helped him in his work from your childhood on. For all the extreme simplicity, even poverty of their lives, the family enjoyed sitting together when the day's work was done, in their ground-floor room at the entrance to the building, where Amm Mahran and his wife would chat together while their child played. His piety made him happy, and the students respected him. The only entertainment he knew was making pilgrimage to the home of Sheikh Ali al-Junaydi, and it was through your father that you came to know the house. "Come along," he'd say, "and I'll show you how to have more fun than playing in the fields. You'll see how sweet life can be, what it's like in an atmosphere of godliness.

It'll give you a sense of peace and contentment, the finest thing you can achieve in life."

The Sheikh greeted you with that sweet and kindly look of his. And how enchanted you were by his fine white beard! "So this is your son you were telling me about," he said to your father. "There's a lot of intelligence in his eyes. His heart is as spotless as yours. You'll find he'll turn out, with God's will, a truly good man." Yes, you really adored Sheikh Ali al-Junaydi, attracted by the purity in his face and the love in his eyes. And those songs and chants of his had delighted you even before your heart was purified by love.

"Tell this boy what it's his duty to do," your father said to the Sheikh one day.

The Sheikh had gazed down at you and said, "We continue learning from the cradle to the grave, but at least start out, Said, by keeping close account of yourself and making sure that from whatever action you initiate some good comes to someone."

Yes, you certainly followed his counsel as best you could, though you only brought it to complete fulfillment when you took up burglary!

The days passed like dreams. And then your good father disappeared, suddenly gone, in a way that a boy simply could not comprehend, and that seemed to baffle even Sheikh Ali himself. How shocked you were that morning, shaking your head and rubbing your eyes to clear away the sleep, awakened by your mother's screams and tears in the little room at the entrance to the student's hostel! You wept with fear and frustration at your helplessness. That evening, however, Rauf Ilwan, at that time a student in law school, had shown how very capable he was. Yes, he was impressive all right, no matter what the circumstances, and you loved him as you did Sheikh Ali, perhaps even more. It was he who later worked hard to have you—or you and your mother, to be more precise—take over Father's job as custodian for the building. Yes, you took on responsibilities at an early age.

And then your mother died. You almost died yourself during your mother's illness, as Rauf Ilwan must surely remember, from that unforgettable day when she had hemorrhaged and you had rushed her to the nearest hospital, the Sabir Hospital, standing like a castle amidst beautiful grounds, where you found yourself and your mother in a reception hall at an entrance more luxurious than anything you could ever have imagined possible. The entire place seemed forbidding, even hostile, but you were in the direst need of help, immediate help.

As the famous doctor was coming out of a room, they mentioned his name and you raced toward him in your gallabiya and sandals, shouting, "My mother! The blood!"

The man had fixed you in a glassy, disapproving stare and had glanced where your mother was lying, stretched out in her filthy dress on a soft couch, a foreign nurse standing nearby, observing the scene. Then the doctor had simply disappeared, saying nothing. The nurse jabbered something in a language you did not understand, though you sensed she was expressing sympathy for your tragedy. At that point, for all your youth, you flew into a real adult's rage, screaming and cursing in protest, smashing a chair to the floor with a crash, so the veneer wood on its back broke in pieces. A horde of servants had appeared and you'd soon found yourself and your mother alone in the tree-lined road outside. A month later your mother had died in the Kasr al-Aini Hospital.

All the time she lay close to death she never released your hand, refusing to take her eyes off you. It was during that long month of illness, however, that you stole for the first time—from the country boy resident in the hostel, who'd accused you without any investigation and was beating you vigorously when Rauf Ilwan turned up and freed you, settling the matter without any further complications. You were a true human being then, Rauf, and you were my teacher, too.

Alone with you, Rauf had said quietly, "Don't you worry. The fact is, I consider this theft perfectly justified. Only you'll find the police watching for you, and the judge won't be lenient with you," he'd added ominously with bitter sarcasm, "however convincing your motives, because he, too, will be protecting himself. Isn't it justice," he'd shouted, "that what is taken by theft should be retrieved by theft? Here I am studying, away from home and family, suffering daily from hunger and deprivation!"

Where have all your principles gone now, Rauf? Dead, no doubt, like my father and my mother, and like my wife's fidelity.

You had no alternative but to leave the students' hostel and seek a living somewhere else. So you waited under the lone palm tree at the end of the green plot until Nabawiyya came and you sprang toward her, saying, "Don't be afraid. I must speak to you. I'm leaving to get a better job. I love you. Don't ever forget me. I love you and always will. And I'll prove I can make you happy and give you a respectable home." Yes, those had been times when sorrows could be forgotten, wounds could be healed, and hope could bring forth fruit from adversity.

All you graves out there, immersed in the gloom, don't jeer at my memories!

He sat up on the sofa, still in the dark, addressing Rauf Ilwan just as though he could see him standing in front of him. "You should have agreed to get me a job writing for your newspaper, you scoundrel. I'd have published our mutual reminiscences there, I'd have shut off your false light good and proper." Then he wondered aloud: "How am I going to stand it here in the dark till Nur comes back near dawn?"

Suddenly he was attacked by an irresistible urge to leave the house and take a walk in the dark. In an instant, his resistance crumbled, collapsing like a building ready to give way; soon he was moving stealthily out of the house. He set off toward Sharia Masani and from there turned toward open wasteland.

Leaving his hideout made him all the more conscious of being hunted. He now knew how mice and foxes feel, slipping away on the run. Alone in the dark, he could see the city's lights glimmering in the distance, lying in wait for him. He quaffed his sense of being alone, until it intoxicated him, then walked on, winding up at last in his old seat next to Tarzan in the coffeehouse. The only other person inside apart from the waiter was an arms smuggler, although outside, a little lower down, at the foot of the hill, the sounds of people talking could be heard.

The waiter brought him some tea at once and then Tarzan leaned over. "Don't spend more than one night in the same place," he whispered.

The smuggler added his advice: "Move way up the Nile."

"But I don't know anyone up there," Said objected.

"You know," the smuggler went on, "I've heard many people express their admiration for you."

"And the police?" Tarzan said heatedly. "Do they admire him, too?"

The smuggler laughed so hard that his whole body shook, as if he were mounted on a camel at the gallop. "Nothing impresses the police," he said at last, when he'd recovered his breath.

"Absolutely nothing," agreed Said.

"But what harm is there in stealing from the rich anyway?" the waiter asked with feeling.

Said beamed as if he were receiving a compliment at some public reception in his honor. "Yes," he said, "but the newspapers have tongues longer than a hangman's rope. And what good does being liked by the people do if the police loathe you?"

Suddenly Tarzan got up, moved to the window, stared outside, looking to left and right, then came back. "I thought I saw a face staring in at us," he reported, clearly worried.

Said's eyes glinted as they darted back and forth between window and door and the waiter went outside to investigate.

"You're always seeing things that aren't there," the smuggler said.

Enraged, Tarzan yelled at him, "Shut up, will you! You seem to think a hangman's rope is some sort of a joke!"

Said left the coffeehouse. Clutching the revolver in his pocket, walking off into the open darkness, he looked cautiously around him, listening as he went. His consciousness of fear, of being alone and hunted, was even stronger now and he knew he must not underestimate his enemies, fearful themselves, but so eager to catch him that they would not rest till they saw him a corpse, laid out and still.

As he neared the house in Sharia Najm al-Din he saw light in Nur's window. It gave him a sense of security for the first time since he'd left the coffeehouse. He found her lying down and wanted to caress her, but it was obvious from her face that she was terribly tired. Her eyes were red. Clearly, something was wrong. He sat down at her feet.

"Please tell me what's wrong, Nur," he said.

"I'm worn out," she said weakly. "I've vomited so much I'm exhausted."

"Was it drink?"

"I've been drinking all my life," she said, her eyes brimming with tears.

This was the first time Said had seen her cry and he was deeply moved. "What was the reason, then?" he said.

"They beat me!"

"The police?"

"No, some young louts, probably students, when I asked them to pay the bill."

Said was touched. "Why not wash your face," he said, "and drink some water?"

"A little later. I'm too tired now."

"The dogs!" Said muttered, tenderly caressing her leg.

"The fabric for the uniform," Nur said, pointing to a parcel on the other sofa. He made a gesture with his hand affectionately and in gratitude.

"I can't look very attractive for you tonight," she said almost apologetically.

"It's not your fault. Just wash your face and get some sleep."

Up in the graveyard heights a dog barked and Nur let out a long, audible sigh. "And she said, 'You have such a rosy future!' " she murmured sadly.

"Who?"

"A fortune-teller. She said there'd be security, peace of mind." Said stared out at the blackness of night piled up outside the window as she went on: "When will that ever be? It's been such a long wait, and all so useless. I have a girlfriend, a little older than me, who always says we'll become just bones or even worse than that, so that even dogs will loathe us." Her voice seemed to come from the very grave and so depressed Said that he could find nothing to say in reply. "Some fortune-teller!" she said. "When is she going to start telling the truth? Where is there any security? I just want to sleep safe and secure, wake up feeling good, and have a quiet, pleasant time. Is that so impossible—for him who raised the Seven Heavens?"

You, too, used to dream of a life like that, but it's all been spent climbing up drainpipes, jumping down from roofs, and being chased in the dark, with badly aimed bullets killing innocent people.

"You need to get some sleep," he told her, thoroughly depressed.

"What I need is a promise," she said. "A promise from the fortune-teller. And that day will come."

"Good."

"You're treating me like a child," she said angrily.

"Never."

"That day really will come!"

TWELVE

Nur watched him as he tried on the uniform, staring at him in surprised delight, until he'd done up the last button. Then, after a moment or two, she said, "Do be sensible. I couldn't bear to lose you again."

"This was a good idea," Said said, displaying his work and examining his reflection in the mirror. "I suppose I'd better be satisfied with the rank of captain!"

By the next evening, however, she'd heard all about his recent dramatic adventure and seen pictures of him in a copy of a weekly magazine belonging to one of her transient male companions. She broke down in front of him. "You've killed someone!" she said, letting out the words with a wail of despair. "How terrible! Didn't I plead with you?"

"But it happened before we met," he said, caressing her.

She looked away. "You don't love me," she said wanly. "I know that. But at least we could have lived together until you did love me!"

"But we can still do that."

"What's the use," she said, almost crying, "when you've committed murder?"

"We can run away together," Said said with a reassuring grin. "It's easy."

"What are we waiting for, then?"

"For the storm to blow over."

Nur stamped her foot in frustration. "But I've heard that there are troops blocking all the exits from Cairo, as if you were the first murderer ever!"

The newspapers! Said thought. All part of the secret war! But he hid his feelings and showed her only his outward calm. "I'll get away all right," he said, "as soon as I decide to. You'll see." Pretending a sudden rage, he gripped her by the hair and snarled: "Don't you know yet who Said Mahran is? All the papers are talking about him! You still don't believe in him? Listen to me; we'll live together forever. And you'll see what the fortune-teller told you come true!"

Next evening, escaping from his loneliness and hoping for news, he slipped out again to Tarzan's coffeehouse, but as soon as he appeared in the doorway Tarzan hurried over and took him out into the open, some distance off. "Please, don't be angry with me," he said apologetically. "Even my café is no longer safe for you."

"But I thought the storm had died down now," Said said, the darkness hiding his concern.

"No. It's getting worse all the time. Because of the newspapers. Go into hiding. But forget about trying to get out of Cairo for a while."

"Don't the papers have anything to go on about but Said Mahran?"

"They made such a lot of noise to everyone about

your past raids that they've got all the government forces in the area stirred up against you." Said got up to leave. "We can meet again—outside the café—anytime you wish," Tarzan remarked as they said goodbye.

So Said went back to his hideout in Nur's house—the solitude, the dark, the waiting—where he suddenly found himself roaring, "It's you, Rauf, you're behind all this!" By this time, all the papers had dropped his case, all except *Al-Zahra*. It was still busy raking up the past, goading the police; by trying so hard to kill him, in fact, it was making a national hero of him. Rauf Ilwan would never rest until the noose was around his neck, and Rauf had all the forces of repression: the law.

And you. Does your ruined life have any meaning at all unless it is to kill your enemies—Ilish Sidra, whereabouts unknown, and Rauf Ilwan, in his mansion of steel? What meaning will there have been to your life if you fail to teach your enemies a lesson? No power on earth will prevent the punishing of the dogs! That's right! No power on earth!

"Rauf Ilwan," Said pleaded aloud, "tell me how it is that time can bring such terrible changes to people!" *Not just a revolutionary student, but revolution personified as a student. Your stirring voice, pitching itself downward toward my ears as I sat at my father's feet in the courtyard of the building, with a force to awaken the very soul. And you'd talk about princes and pashas, transforming those fine gentlemen with your magic into mere thieves. And to see you on Mudiriyya Road, striding out amidst your men you called your equals as they munched their sugarcane in their flowing gallabiyas, when your voice would reach such a pitch that it seemed to flow right over the field and make the palm tree bow before it—unforgettable. Yes, there was a strange power in you that I found nowhere else, not even in Sheikh Ali al-Junaydi.*

That's how you were, Rauf. To you alone goes the credit for my father's enrolling me in school. You'd roar with delighted laughter at my successes. "Do you see now?" you'd say to my father. "You didn't even want him to get an education. Just you look at those eyes of his; he's going to shake things to their foundations!" You taught me to love reading. You discussed everything with me, as if I were your equal. I was one of your listeners—at the foot of the same tree where the history of my love began—and the times themselves were listening to you, too: "The people! Theft! The holy fire! The rich! Hunger! Justice!"

The day you were imprisoned you rose up in my eyes to the very sky, higher still when you protected me the first time I stole, when your remarks about theft gave me back my self-respect. Then there was the time you told me sadly, "There's no real point in isolated theft; there has to be organization." After that I never stopped either reading or robbing. It was you who gave me the names of people who deserved to be robbed, and it was in theft that I found my glory, my honor. And I was generous to many people, Ilish Sidra among them.

Said shouted in anger to the darkened room: "Are you really the same one? The Rauf Ilwan who owns a mansion? You're the fox behind the newspaper campaign. You, too, want to kill me, to murder your conscience and the past as well. But I won't die before I've killed you: you're the number one traitor. What nonsense life would turn out to be if I were myself killed tomorrow—in retribution for murdering a man I didn't even know! If there's going to be any meaning to life—and to death, too—I simply have to kill you. My last outburst of rage at the evil of the world. And all those things lying out there in the graveyard below the window will help me. As for the rest, I'll leave it to Sheikh Ali to solve the riddle."

Just when the call to the dawn prayers was announced he heard the door open and Nur came in carrying some grilled meat, drinks, and newspapers. She seemed quite happy, having apparently forgotten her two days of distress and depression, and her presence dispelled his own gloom and exhaustion, made him ready again to embrace what life had to offer: food, drink, and news. She kissed him and, for the first time, he responded spontaneously, with a sense of gratitude, knowing her now to be the person closest to him for as long as he might live. He wished she'd never leave.

He uncorked a bottle as usual, poured himself a glass, and drank it down in one gulp.

"Why didn't you get some sleep?" Nur said, peering closely at his tired face.

Flipping through the newspapers, he made no reply.

"It must be torture to wait in the dark," she said, feeling sorry for him.

"How are things outside?" he asked, tossing the papers aside.

"Just like always." She undressed down to her slip and Said smelled powder moistened with sweat. "People are talking about you," she went on, "as if you were some storybook hero. But they don't have any idea what torture we go through."

"Most Egyptians neither fear nor dislike thieves," said Said as he bit into a piece of meat. Several minutes passed in silence while they ate, then he added: "But they do have an instinctive dislike for dogs."

"Well," said Nur with a smile, licking her fingertips, "I like dogs."

"I don't mean that kind of dog."

"Yes, I always had one at home until I saw the last one die. That made me cry a lot and so I decided not to have one again."

"That's right," said Said. "If love's going to cause problems, just steer clear of it."

"You don't understand me. Or love me."

"Don't be like that," he said, pleading. "Can't you see the whole world is cruel enough and unjust enough as it is?"

Nur drank until she could hardly sit up. Her real name was Shalabiyya, she confessed. Then she told him tales of the old days in Balyana, of her childhood amid the quiet waters, of her youth and how she'd run away. "And my father was the *umda*," she said proudly, "the village headman."

"You mean the *umda*'s servant!" She frowned, but he went on: "Well, that's what you told me first."

Nur laughed so heartily that Said could see bits of parsley caught in her teeth. "Did I really say that?" she asked.

"Yes. And that's what turned Rauf Ilwan into a traitor."

She stared at him uncomprehendingly. "And who's Rauf Ilwan?"

"Don't lie to me," Said snarled. "A man who has to stay in the dark, waiting by himself, a man like that can't stand lies."

THIRTEEN

A little after midnight, with a quarter-moon shining faintly in the west, Said headed off across the wasteland. A hundred yards or so from the café he stopped, whistled three times, and stood waiting, feeling that he had to strike his blow or else go mad, hoping that Tarzan would have some information at last.

When Tarzan appeared, moving like a wave of darkness, they embraced and Said asked him, "What's new?"

"One of them's finally turned up," the stout man replied, out of breath from walking.

"Who?" Said asked anxiously.

"It's Bayaza," said Tarzan, still gripping his hand, "and he's in my place now, clinching a deal."

"So my waiting wasn't wasted. Do you know which way he's going?"

"He'll go back by Jabal Road."

"Thanks very much indeed, friend."

Said left quickly, making his way east, guided by the faint moonlight to the clump of trees around the wells. He moved on along the south side of the grove until he reached its tip, ending in the sands where the road up the mountain began. There he crouched behind a tree and waited.

A cool breeze sent a whisper through the grove. It was a desolate, lonely spot. Gripping his revolver hard, he pondered the chance that might now be at hand, to bear down on his enemy and achieve his long-awaited goal. And then death, a final resting place. "Ilish Sidra," he said aloud, heard only by the trees as they drank in the breeze, "and then Rauf Ilwan. Both in one night. After that, let come what may."

Tense, impatient, he did not have long to wait for a figure to come hurrying in the dark from the direction of the café toward the tip of the woods. When there was only a yard or two left between the man and the road, Said leaped out, leveling his revolver.

"Stop!" he roared.

The man stopped as if hit by a bolt of electricity, and stared at Said speechless.

"Bayaza, I know where you were, what you've been doing, how much cash you're carrying."

The man's breath came forth in a hiss and his arm made a slight, hesitant movement, a twitch. "The money's for my children," he gasped.

Said slapped him hard across the face, making him blink. "You still don't recognize me, Bayaza, you dog!"

"Who are you? I know your voice, but I can't believe . . ." Bayaza said, then cried out, "Said Mahran!"

"Don't move! The first move you make, you're dead."

"You kill me? Why? We've no reason to be enemies."

"Well, here's one," muttered Said, stretching his hand to reach into the man's clothing, locating the heavy purse, and ripping it loose.

"But that's my money. I'm not your enemy."

"Shut up. I haven't got all I want yet."

"But we're old pals. That's something you should respect."

"If you want to live, tell me where Ilish Sidra is staying."

"I don't know," Bayaza replied emphatically. "No one knows."

Said slapped him again, harder than before, "I'll kill you if you don't tell me where he is," he shouted. "And you won't get your money back until I know you're telling the truth!"

"I don't know. I swear I don't know," Bayaza whispered.

"You liar!"

"I'll swear any oath you like!"

"You're telling me he's disappeared completely, dissolved like salt in water?"

"I really don't know. No one knows. He moved out right after your visit, afraid of what you might do. I'm telling the truth. He moved to Rod al-Farag."

"His address?"

"Wait, Said," he pleaded. "And after Shaban Husayn was killed he took his family away again. He didn't tell anyone where. He was scared, all right, and his wife was, too. And no one knows anything more about them."

"Bayaza!"

"I swear I'm telling the truth!" Said hit him again, and the man groaned with pain and fear. "Why are you beating me, Said? God damn Sidra wherever he may be; is he my brother or my father that I would die on his account?"

At last, and reluctantly, Said believed him and began to lose hope of ever finding his enemy. If only he wasn't a hunted man, wanted for murder, he would bide his time and wait patiently for the proper opportunity! But that misdirected shot of his had struck at the heart of his own most intense desire.

"You're being unfair to me," said Bayaza. When Said did not reply, he went on: "And what about my money? I never harmed you." He held a hand to the side of his face where Said had struck him. "And you've no right to take my money. We used to work together!"

"And you were always one of Sidra's buddies, too."

"Yes, I was his friend and his partner, but that doesn't mean I'm your enemy. I had nothing to do with what he did to you."

The fight was over now and a retreat was the only course. "Well," Said told him, "I'm in need of some cash."

"Take what you like, then," said Bayaza.

Said was satisfied with ten pounds. The other man

left, dazed, as if he scarcely believed his escape, and Said found himself alone again in the desert, the light from the moon brighter now and the whispering of the trees harsher. So Ilish Sidra has slipped out of his clutches, escaped his due punishment, rescued his own treacherous self, adding one to the number of scot-free traitors. Rauf, the only hope I have left is in you, that you won't make me lose my life in vain.

FOURTEEN

By the time Said had returned to the flat, dressed in his officer's uniform, and left, it was well after one o'clock. He turned toward Abbasiyya Street, avoiding the lights and forcing himself to walk very naturally, then took a taxi to Gala's Bridge, passing an unpleasant number of policemen en route.

At the dock near the bridge he rented a small rowboat for two hours and promptly set off in it south, toward Rauf Ilwan's house. It was a fine starry night, a cool breeze blowing, the quarter-moon still visible in the clear sky above the trees along the riverbank. Excited, full of energy, Said felt ready to spring into vigorous action. Ilish Sidra's escape was not a defeat, not as long as punishment was about to descend on Rauf Ilwan. For Rauf, after all, personified the highest standard of treachery, from which people like Ilish and Nabawiyya and all the other traitors on earth sought inspiration.

"It's time to settle accounts, Rauf," he said, pulling hard on the oars. "And if anyone but the police stood as judges between us, I'd teach you a lesson in front of everyone. They, the people, everyone—all the people except the real robbers—are on my side, and that's what will console me in my everlasting perdition. I am, in fact, your soul. You've sacrificed me. I lack organization, as you would put it. I now understand many of the things you used to say that I couldn't comprehend then. And the worst of it is that despite this support from millions of people I find myself driven away into dismal isolation, with no one to help. It's senseless, all of it, a waste. No bullet could clear away its absurdity. But at least a bullet will be right, a bloody protest, something to comfort the living and the dead, to let them hold on to their last shred of hope."

At a point opposite the big house, he turned shoreward, rowed in to the bank, jumped out, pulled the boat up after him until its bow was well up on dry land, then climbed the bank up to the road, where, feeling calm and secure in his officer's uniform, he walked away. The road seemed empty and when he got to the house he saw no sign of guards, which both pleased and angered him. The house itself was shrouded in darkness except for a single light at the entrance, convincing him that the owner was not yet back, that forced entry was unnecessary, and that a number of other difficulties had been removed.

Walking quite casually, he turned down the street along the left side of the house and followed it to its end at Sharia Giza, then he turned along Sharia Giza and proceeded to the other street, passing along the right side of the house, until he regained the riverside, examining everything along the way most carefully. Then he made his way over to a patch of ground shaded from the streetlights by a tree, and stood waiting, his eyes fixed on the house, relaxing them only by gazing out from time to time at the dark surface of the river; his thoughts fled to Rauf's treachery, the deception that had crushed his life, the ruin that was facing him, the death blocking his path, all the things that made Rauf's death an absolute necessity. He watched each car with bated breath as it approached.

Finally one of them stopped before the gate of the house, which was promptly opened by the doorkeeper, and Said darted into the street to the left of the house, keeping close to the wall, stopping at a point opposite the entrance, while the car moved slowly down the drive. It came to a halt in front of the entrance, where the light that had been left on illuminated the whole entranceway. Said took out his revolver now and aimed it carefully as the car door opened and Rauf Ilwan got out.

"Rauf!" Said bellowed. As the man turned in shock toward the source of this shout, Said yelled again: "This is Said Mahran! Take that!"

But before he could fire, a shot from within the garden, whistling past him very close, disturbed his aim. He fired and ducked to escape the next shot, then raised his head in desperate determination, took aim, and fired again.

All this happened in an instant. After one more wild, hasty shot, he sped away as fast as he could run toward the river, pushed the boat out into the water, and leapt into it, rowing toward the opposite bank.

Unknown sources deep within him released immediate reserves of physical strength, but his thoughts and emotions swirled as though caught in a whirlpool. He seemed to sense shots being fired, voices of people gathering, and a sudden loss of power in some part of his body, but the distance between the riverbanks was small at that point and he reached the other side, quickly leapt ashore, leaving the boat to drift in the water, and climbed up to the street, clutching the gun in his pocket.

Despite his confused emotions, he proceeded carefully and calmly, looking neither to the right nor to the left. Aware of people rushing down to the water's edge behind him, of confused shouts from the direction of a bridge, and a shrill whistle piercing the night air, he expected a pursuer to accost him at any moment, and he was ready to put all his efforts into either bluffing his way out or entering one last battle. Before anything else could happen, however, a taxi cruised by. He hailed it and climbed in; the piercing pain he felt as soon as he sat back on the seat was nothing compared to the relief of being safe again.

He crept up to Nur's flat in complete darkness and stretched out on one of the sofas, still in his uniform. The pain returned now, and he identified its source, a little above his knee, where he put his hand and felt a sticky liquid, with sharper pain. Had he knocked against something? Or was it a bullet, when he'd been behind the wall perhaps, or running? Pressing fingers all around the wound, he determined that it was only a scratch; if it had been a bullet, it must have grazed him without penetrating.

He got up, took off his uniform, felt for his nightshirt on the sofa, and put it on. Then he walked around the flat testing out the leg, remembering how once he'd run down Sharia Muhammad Ali with a bullet lodged in the leg. "Why, you're capable of miracles," he told himself. "You'll get away all right. With a little coffee powder this wound will bind up nicely."

But had he managed to kill Rauf Ilwan? And who had shot at him from inside the garden? *Let's hope you didn't hit some other poor innocent fellow like before. And Rauf must surely have been killed—you never miss, as you used to demonstrate in target practice out in the desert beyond the hill. Yes, now you can write a letter to the papers: "Why I Killed Rauf Ilwan." That will give back the meaning your life has lost: the bullet that killed Rauf Ilwan will at the same time have destroyed your sense of loss, of waste. A world without morals is like a universe without gravity. I want nothing, long for nothing more than to die a death that has some meaning to it.*

Nur came home worn out, carrying food and drink. She kissed him as usual and smiled a greeting, but her eyes suddenly fastened on his uniform trousers. She put her parcel on the sofa, picked them up, and held them out to him.

"There's blood!" she said.

Said noticed it for the first time. "It's just a minor

wound," he said, showing her his leg. "I hit it on the door of a taxi."

"You've been out in that uniform for some specific reason! There's no limit to your madness. You'll kill me with worry!"

"A little bit of coffee powder will cure this wound even before the sun rises."

"My soul rises, you mean! You are simply murdering me! Oh, when will this nightmare end?"

In a burst of nervous energy Nur dressed the wound with powdered coffee, then bound it up with a cutting from fabric she was using to make a dress, complaining about her ill-fortune all the time she worked.

"Why don't you take a shower?" said Said. "It'll make you feel good."

"You don't know good from bad," she said, leaving the room.

By the time she came back to the bedroom, he had already drunk a third of a bottle of wine and his mood and nerves felt much improved.

"Drink up!" he said as she sat down. "After all, I'm here, all right, in a nice safe place, way out of sight of the police."

"I'm really very depressed," Nur whimpered, combing her wet hair.

"Who can determine the future anyway?" he said, taking a swallow.

"Only our own actions can."

"Nothing, absolutely nothing is certain. Except your being with me, and that's something I can't do without."

"So you say now!"

"And I've got more to say. Being with you, after being out there with bullets tearing after me, is like being in Paradise." Her long sigh in response was deep, as if in self-communion at night; and he went on: "You really are very good to me. I want you to know I'm grateful."

"But I'm so worried. All I want is for you to be safe."

"We'll still have our opportunity."

"Escape! Put your mind to how we can escape."

"Yes, I will. But let's wait for the dogs to close their eyes a while."

"But you go outside so carelessly. You're obsessed with killing your wife and this other man. You won't kill them. But you will bring about your own destruction."

"What did you hear in town?"

"The taxi driver who brought me home was on your side. But he said you'd killed some poor innocent fellow."

Said grunted irritably and forestalled any expression of regret by taking another big swallow, gesturing at Nur to drink, too. She raised the glass to her lips.

"What else did you hear?" he said.

"On the houseboat where I spent the evening one

man said you act as a stimulant, a diversion to relieve people's boredom."

"And what did you reply?"

"Nothing at all," Nur said, pouting. "But I do defend you, and you don't look after yourself at all. You don't love me either. But to me you're more precious than my life itself; I've never in my whole life known happiness except in your arms. But you'd rather destroy yourself than love me." She was crying now, the glass still in her hand.

Said put his arm around her. "You'll find me true to my promise," he whispered. "We will escape and live together forever."

FIFTEEN

What enormous headlines and dramatic photos! It was obviously the major news item. Rauf Ilwan had been interviewed and had said that Said Mahran had been a servant in the students' hostel when he'd lived there, that he'd felt very sorry for him, and that later, after his release from prison, Said had visited him to ask for help, so he'd given him some money to start a new life; that Said had tried to rob his house the very same night and that he, Rauf, had caught and scolded him, but let him go out of compassion. And that then Said had come back to kill him!

The papers accused Said of being mad, craving for power and blood: his wife's infidelity had made him lose his mind, they said, and now he was killing at random. Rauf had apparently been untouched, but the unfortunate doorkeeper had fallen. Another poor innocent killed!

"Damnation!" cursed Said as he read the news.

The hue and cry was deafening now.

A huge reward was offered to anyone giving information of his whereabouts, and articles warned people against any sympathy for him. Yes, he thought, you're the top story today, all right. *And you'll be the top story until you're dead. You're a source of fear and fascination—like some freak of nature—and all those people choking with boredom owe their pleasure to you. As for your gun, it's obvious that it will kill only the innocent. You'll be its last victim.*

"Is this madness, then?" he asked himself, choking on the question.

Yes, you always wanted to cause a real stir, even if you were only a clown. Your triumphant raids on the homes of the rich were like wine, intoxicating your pride-filled head. And those words of Rauf that you believed, even though he did not—it was they that really chopped off your head, that killed you dead!

He was alone in the night. There was still some wine in a bottle, which he drank down to the last drop. As he stood in the dark, enveloped in the silence of the neighboring graves, slightly giddy, he began to feel that he would indeed overcome all his difficulties, that he could disdain death. The sound of mysterious music within him delighted him.

"A misdirected bullet has made of me the man of the hour!" he declared to the dark.

Through the window shutters he looked over the cemetery, at the graves lying there quiet in the moonlight.

"Hey, all you judges out there, listen well to me," he said. "I've decided to offer my own defense for myself."

Back in the center of the room he took off his

nightshirt. The room was hot, the wine had raised his body heat. His wound throbbed beneath the bandage, but the pain convinced him it was beginning to heal.

"I'm not like the others," he said, staring into the dark, "who have stood on this stand before. You must give special consideration to the education of the accused. But the truth is, there's no difference between me and you except that I'm on the stand and you're not. And that difference is only incidental, of no real importance at all. But what's truly ridiculous is that the distinguished teacher of the accused is a treacherous scoundrel. You may well be astonished at this fact. It can happen, however, that the cord carrying current to a lamp is dirty, speckled with fly shit."

He turned to a sofa and lay down on it. In the distance he could hear a dog barking. *How can you ever convince your judges, when there is a personal animosity between you and them that has nothing to do with the so-called public welfare? They're kin to the scoundrel after all, whereas there's a whole century of time between you and them. You must then ask the victim to bear witness. You must assert that the treachery has become a silent conspiracy: "I did not kill the servant of Rauf Ilwan. How could I kill a man I did not know and who didn't know me? Rauf Ilwan's servant was killed because, quite simply, he was the servant of Rauf Ilwan. Yesterday his spirit visited me and I jumped to hide in shame, but he pointed out to me that millions of people are killed by mistake and without due cause."*

Yes, these words will glitter; they'll be crowned with a

not-guilty verdict. You are sure of what you say. And apart from that, they will believe, deep down, that your profession is lawful, a profession of gentlemen at all times and everywhere, that the truly false values—yes!—are those that value your life in pennies and your death at a thousand pounds. The judge over on the left is winking at you; cheer up!

"I will always seek the head of Rauf Ilwan, even as a last request from the hangman, even before seeing my daughter. I am forced not to count my life in days. A hunted man only feeds on new excitements, which pour down upon him in the span of his solitude like rain."

The verdict will be no more cruel that Sana's cold shyness toward you. She killed you before the hangman could. And even the sympathy of the millions for you is voiceless, impotent, like the longings of the dead. Will they not forgive the gun its error, when it is their most elevated master?

"Whoever kills me will be killing the millions. I am the hope and the dream, the redemption of cowards; I am good principles, consolation, the tears that recall the weeper to humility. And the declaration that I'm mad must encompass all who are loving. Examine the causes of this insane occasion, then reach your judgment however you wish!"

His dizziness increased.

Then the verdict came down: that he was a great man, truly great in every sense of the word. His greatness might be momentarily shrouded in black, from a community of sympathy with all those graves out there, but the glory of his greatness would live on, even after death. Its fury was blessed by the force that flowed through the roots of plants, the cells of animals, and the hearts of men.

Eventually sleep overtook him, though he only knew it when he awoke to find light filling the room and he saw Nur standing looking down at him. Her eyes were dead tired, her lower lip drooped, and her shoulders slumped. She looked the very picture of despair. He knew in an instant what the trouble was; she'd heard about his latest exploit and it had shocked her deeply.

"You are even more cruel than I imagined," she said. "I just don't understand you. But for heaven's sake have mercy and kill me, too." He sat up on the sofa, but made no reply. "You're busy thinking how to kill, not how to escape, and you'll be killed, too. Do you imagine you can defeat the whole government, with its troops filling the streets?"

"Sit down and let's discuss it calmly."

"How can I be calm? And what are we to discuss? Everything's over now. Just kill me, too, for mercy's sake!"

"I don't ever want harm to come to you," he said quietly and in a tender tone of voice.

"I'll never believe a word you say. Why do you murder doorkeepers?"

"I didn't mean to harm him!" he said angrily.

"And the other one? Who is this Rauf Ilwan? What is your relationship with him? Was he involved with your wife?"

"What a ridiculous idea," he said, laughing so drily it was like a cough. "No, there are other reasons. He's a traitor, too, but of another sort. I can't explain it all to you."

"But you can torture me to death."

"As I just said, sit down so we can talk calmly."

"You're still in love with your wife, that bitch, but you want to put me through hell all the same."

"Nur," he pleaded, "please don't torture me. I'm terribly depressed."

Nur stopped talking, affected by a distress she could never have seen in him before. "I feel as if the most precious thing in my whole life is about to die," she said at last, sadly.

"That's just your imagination, your fear. Gamblers like me never admit to setbacks. I'll remind you of that sometime."

"When will that be?" she asked quietly.

"Oh, sooner than you think," Said replied, pretending boundless self-confidence.

He leaned toward her and pulled her down by the hand. He pressed his face against hers, his nose filling with the smell of wine and sweat. But he felt no disgust and kissed her with genuine tenderness.

SIXTEEN

Dawn was close, but Nur had not returned—though the waiting and all his worry had exhausted him, bouts of insomnia kept crushing against his brain—and now the warm darkness was splitting apart to reveal one flaming question: Was it possible that the promised reward was having some effect on Nur?

Suspicion had tainted his blood to the last drop now: he had visions of infidelity as pervasive as dust in a windstorm. He remembered how sure he was once that Nabawiyya belonged to him, when in reality she'd probably never loved him at all, even in the days of the lone palm tree at the edge of the field.

But surely Nur would never betray him, never turn him over to the police for the reward. She had no interest now in such financial transactions. She was getting on in life. What she wanted was a sincere emotional relationship with someone. He ought to feel guilty for his suspicious thoughts.

The worry over Nur's absence persisted, nevertheless. It's your hunger, thirst, and all the waiting that's getting you down, he said to himself. *Just like that time you stood waiting beneath the palm tree, waiting for Nabawiyya, and she didn't come. You began prowling around the old Turkish woman's house, biting your fingernails with im-*

patience and so crazy with worry you almost knocked on her door. And what a quiver of joy when she did emerge—a feeling of complete exhilaration, spreading through you, lifting you up to the seventh heaven.

It had been a time of tears and laughter, of uncontrolled emotion, a time of confidence, a time of boundless joy. Don't think about the palm tree days now. They're gone forever, cut off by blood, bullets, and madness. Think only about what you've got to do now, waiting here, filled with bitterness, in this murderous stifling darkness.

He could only conclude that Nur did not want to come back, did not want to save him from the tortures of solitude in the dark, from hunger and thirst. At the height of a bout of remorse and despair, he at last fell asleep. When he opened his eyes again he saw daylight and felt the heat slipping through the shutters into the closed room. Worried and confused, he stepped quickly into the bedroom, to find it exactly as Nur had left it the day before, then roamed around the entire flat. Nur had not returned. Where, he wondered, could she have spent the night? What had prevented her return? And how long was he to be sentenced to this solitary confinement?

He was feeling distinct pangs of hunger now, despite his worries, and he went into the kitchen. On the unwashed plates there he found several scraps of bread, bits of meat sticking to bones, and some parsley. He consumed them all, ravenously gnawing on the bones like a dog, then spent the rest of the whole day wondering why she had not returned, wondering if she ever would. He would sit for a while, then wander about and sit again. His only distraction was gazing through the shutters out over the cemetery, watching the funerals and aimlessly counting the graves. Evening came, but Nur had still not returned.

There must be some sort of reason. Wherever could she be? He felt his worry, anger, and hunger tearing him apart. Nur was in trouble, there was no doubt of that, but somehow she simply had to free herself from her difficulty, whatever it was, and come back. Otherwise what would become of him?

After midnight he quietly left the flat and made his way over the waste ground to Tarzan's coffeehouse. He whistled three times when he arrived at the spot they'd agreed on and waited until Tarzan came out.

"Do be extremely careful," said Tarzan, shaking his hand, "there are agents watching everywhere."

"I need some food!"

"You don't say! You're hungry, then!"

"Yes. Nothing ever surprises you, does it?"

"I'll send the waiter to get you some cooked meat. But I'm telling you, it really is dangerous for you to go out."

"Oh, we had worse trouble in the old days, you and I."

"I don't think so. That last attack of yours has turned the whole world upside down on top of you."

"It's always been upside down."

"But it was disastrous of you to attack a man of importance!"

They parted and Said withdrew a little. After some time the food was brought him and he gulped it down, sitting on the sand beneath a moon now really full. He looked over at the light coming from Tarzan's café on the little hill and imagined the customers sitting there in the room chatting. No, he really did not like being alone. When he was with others his stature seemed to grow giantlike: he had a talent for friendship, leadership, even heroism. Without all that there was simply no spice to life. But had Nur come back yet? Would she return at all? Would he go back to find her there or would there be more of that murderous loneliness?

At last he got up, brushed the sand and dust from his trousers, and walked off toward the grove, planning to go back to the flat by the path that wound around the south side of the Martyr's Tomb. Near the tip of the grove, at the spot where he'd waylaid Bayaza, the earth seemed to split open, emitting two figures who jumped out on either side of him.

"Stop where you are!" said one of them in a deep urbanized country accent.

"And let's see your identity card!" barked the other.

The former shone a flashlight into his face and Said lowered his head as though to protect his eyes, demanding angrily, "Who do you think you are? Come on, answer me!"

They were taken aback by his imperious tone; they'd now seen his uniform in the glow of the flashlight.

"I'm very sorry indeed, sir," the first man said. "In the shadow of the trees we couldn't see who you were."

"And who are you?" Said shouted, with even more anger in his voice.

"We're from the station at al-Waily, sir," they answered hastily.

The flashlight was turned off now, but Said had already seen something disturbing in the expression of the second man, who had been peering very quizzically at him, as though suddenly filled with doubt. Afraid he might lose control of the situation, Said moved decisively and with force, swinging a fist into both their bellies. They reeled back, and before they could recover he sent a hail of blows at chins and bellies until they were unconscious. Then he dashed away as fast as he could go. At the corner of Sharia Najm al-Din he stopped to make sure no one was following, then he continued along quietly to the flat.

Once there he found it as empty as when he'd left, with only more loneliness, boredom, and worry there to meet him. He took off his jacket and threw himself onto a sofa in the dark. His own sad voice came to him audibly: "Nur, where are you?"

All was not well with her, that was obvious. Had the police arrested her? Had some louts attacked her? She had to be in some sort of trouble. Emotions and instincts told him that much, and that he would never see Nur again. The thought choked him with despair, not merely because he would soon lose a safe hiding place but also because he knew he'd lost affection and companionship as well. He saw her there in the dark before him—Nur, with all her smiles and joking, her love and her unhappiness—and the terrible depression he felt made him aware that she had penetrated much deeper within him than he had imagined, that she had become a part of him, and that she should never have been separated from this life of his which was in shreds and tottering on the brink of an abyss. Closing his eyes in the darkness, he silently acknowledged that he did love her and that he would not hesitate to give his own life to bring her safely back. Then one thought made him growl in anger: "And yet would her demise cause so much as a single ripple anywhere?"

No, definitely not. Not even a pretense of grief would be made for the loss of Nur, who was only a woman with no protector, adrift on a sea of waves either indifferent or hostile. And Sana, too, might well find herself one day with no one to look after her. These thoughts scared and angered him and he gripped his gun and pointed it in front of him in the dark, as though warning the unknown. In deep despair, delirious in the silence and dark, he began to sob; and sobbed until late in the night sleep finally overcame him.

It was daylight when he next opened his eyes, aware that someone's knocking on the door had awakened him. He jumped up in alarm and tiptoed to the front door of the flat, the knocking continuing all the time.

"Madame Nur! Madame Nur!" a woman's voice shouted.

Who was the woman and what could she want? He got his revolver from the other room. Now he heard a man's voice: "Well, maybe she's gone out."

"No," he heard the woman reply, "at this time of day she's always home. And she's never been late with the rent before."

So it must be the landlady. The woman gave one last angry bang on the door and yelled: "Today's the fifth of the month and I'm not going to wait any longer!"

Then she and the man walked away, grumbling as they went.

Circumstances were after him now, as well as the police. The woman would certainly not wait long and would be sure to get into the flat by one means or another. The best thing for him was to get out as soon as he possibly could.

But where was he to go?

SEVENTEEN

Late in the afternoon and then again during the evening the landlady returned. "No, no, Madame Nur," she muttered as she finally left, "everything has to come to an end sometime, you know."

At midnight Said slipped out. Although his confidence in everything had gone, he was careful to walk very naturally and slowly, as if merely taking a stroll. More than once, when the thought struck him that people passing by or standing around might well be informers, he braced himself for one last desperate battle. After the encounter on the previous day, he had no doubts that the police would be in occupation of the whole area near Tarzan's café, so he moved off toward Jabal Road.

Hunger was tearing at his stomach now. On the road, it occurred to him that Sheikh Ali al-Junaydi's house might well provide a temporary place of refuge while he thought out his next moves. It was only as he slipped into the courtyard of the silent house that he realized that he had left his uniform in the sitting room of Nur's flat. Infuriated by his forgetfulness Said went on into the old man's room, where the lamplight showed the Sheikh sitting in the corner reserved for prayer, completely engrossed in a whispered monologue. Said walked over to the wall where he'd left his books and sat down, exhausted.

The Sheikh continued his quiet utterance until Said addressed him: "Good evening, then, Sheikh Ali."

The old man raised his hand to his head in response to the greeting, but did not break off his incantations.

"Sheikh, I'm really hungry," Said said.

The old man seemed to interrupt his chant, gazed at him vacantly, then nodded with his chin to a side table nearby where Said saw some bread and figs. He got up at once, went to the table, and ravenously consumed it all, then stood there looking at the Sheikh with unappeased eyes.

"Don't you have any money?" the Sheikh said quietly.

"Oh yes."

"Why not go and buy yourself something to eat?"

Said then made his way quietly back to his seat. The Sheikh sat contemplating him for a while, then said, "When are you going to settle down, do you think?"

"Not on the face of this earth."

"That's why you're hungry, even though you've got money."

"So be it, then."

"As for me," the Sheikh commented, "I was just reciting some verses about life's sorrows. I was reciting in a joyful frame of mind."

"Yes. Well, you're certainly a happy Sheikh," Said

said. "The scoundrels have got away," he went on angrily. "How can I settle down after that?"

"How many of them are there?"

"Three."

"What joy for the world if its scoundrels number only three."

"No, there are very many more, but my enemies are only three."

"Well then, no one has 'got away.' "

"I'm not responsible for the world, you know."

"Oh yes. You're responsible for both this world and the next!" While Said puffed in exasperation, the Sheikh continued: "Patience is holy and through it things are blessed."

"But it's the guilty who succeed, while the innocent fail," Said commented glumly.

The Sheikh sighed. "When shall we succeed in achieving peace of mind under the rule of authority?"

"When authority becomes fair," Said replied.

"It is always fair."

Said shook his head angrily. "Yes," he muttered. "They've got away now, all right, damn it." The Sheikh merely smiled without speaking. Said's voice changed its tone as he tried to alter the course of the conversation. "I'm going to sleep with my face toward the wall. I don't want anyone who visits you to see me. I'm going to hide out here with you. Please protect me."

"Trusting God means entrusting one's lodging to God alone," the Sheikh said gently.

"Would you give me up?"

"Oh no, God forbid."

"Would it be in your power, with all the grace with which you're endowed, to save me, then?"

"You can save yourself, if you wish," came the Sheikh's reply.

"I will kill the others," Said whispered to himself, and aloud said, "Are you capable of straightening the shadow of something crooked?"

"I do not concern myself with shadows," the Sheikh replied softly.

Silence followed and light from the moon streamed more strongly through the window onto the ceiling. In a whisper the Sheikh began reciting a mystic chant: "All beauty in creation stems from You."

Yes, Said told himself quietly, the Sheikh will always find something appropriate to say. *But this house of yours, dear sir, is not secure, though you yourself might be security personified. I've got to get away, no matter what the cost. And as for you, Nur, let's hope at least good luck will protect you, if you find neither justice nor mercy. But how did I forget that uniform? I wrapped it up, intending to take it with me. How could I have forgotten it at the last moment? I've lost my touch. From all this sleeplessness, loneliness, dark, and worry. They'll find that uniform. It might supply the first thread leading to you: they'll have dogs smelling it, fanning out in all directions to the very ends of the earth, sniffing and barking to complete a drama that will titillate newspaper readers.*

Suddenly the Sheikh spoke again in a melancholy

tone of voice: "I asked you to raise up your face to the heavens, yet here you are announcing that you are going to turn it to the wall!"

"But don't you remember what I told you about the scoundrels?" Said demanded, gazing at him sadly.

" 'Remember the name of your Lord, if you forget.' "

Said lowered his gaze, feeling troubled, then wondered again, as depression gripped him further, how he could have forgotten the uniform.

The Sheikh said suddenly, as if addressing someone else, "He was asked: 'Do you know of any incantation we can recite or potion we can use that might perhaps nullify a decree of God?' And he answered: 'Such would be a decree of God!' "

"What do you mean?" Said asked.

"Your father was never one to fail to understand my words," replied the old man, sighing sadly.

"Well," Said said irritably, "it is regrettable that I didn't find sufficient food in your home, just as it is unfortunate that I forgot the uniform. Also my mind does fail to comprehend you and I will turn my face to the wall. But I'm confident that I'm in the right."

Smiling sadly, the Sheikh said, "My Master stated: 'I gaze in the mirror many times each day fearing that my face might have turned black!' "

"You?!"

"No, my Master himself."

"How," Said asked scornfully, "could the scoundrels keep checking in the mirror every hour?"

The Sheikh bowed his head, reciting, "All beauty in creation stems from You."

Said closed his eyes, saying to himself, "I'm really tired, but I'll have no peace until I get that uniform back."

EIGHTEEN

At last exhaustion conquered his will. He forgot his determination to get the uniform and fell asleep, awaking a little before midday. Knowing he would have to wait until nightfall to move, he spent the time setting out a plan for his escape, fully aware that any major step would have to be put off for a while, until the police relaxed their surveillance of the area near Tarzan's café. Tarzan was the very pivot of the plan.

Sometime after midnight he entered Sharia Najm al-Din. There was light coming from a window of the flat. He stood staring up at it in amazement, and when he finally believed what he saw, his heart seemed to beat so loudly as almost to deafen him, while a wave of elation roared over him, sweeping him out of a nightmare world. Nur was in the flat! Where had she been? Why had she been away? At least she was back now. And she must be suffering the scorch of those same hellfires where he'd been burning, wondering where he was. He knew she was back by that instinct of his that had never deceived him, and the strain of being on the run would now recede for a while, perhaps for good. He would hold her tight in his arms, pouring out his eternal love for her.

Intoxicated with joy and assured of success, he crept into the building and climbed the stairs, dreaming of one victory after another. There was no limit to what he could do. He would get away and settle down for a long time, then come back eventually and deal with those scoundrels.

A little out of breath, he came up to the door. *I love you, Nur. With all my heart I do love you, twice as much as you have loved me. In your breast I will bury all my misery, the treachery of those scoundrels and my daughter's alarm.* He knocked on the door.

It opened to reveal a man he had never seen before, a little man in his underclothes, who stared back at him in astonishment and said, "Yes; what can I do for you?"

The little man's look of inquiry soon gave way to one of confusion and then alarm. Dumbfounded, certain he'd recognized him, Said silenced him instantly, slamming one fist into his mouth and the other into his stomach. As he lowered the body quietly to the threshold, Said thought of entering to search for his uniform, but he couldn't be sure the flat was empty. Then from inside he heard a woman's voice calling, "Who was that at the door, dear?"

It was hopeless. Said turned and raced back down the stairs and out into the street, then made his way up Sharia Masani to Jabal Road, where he could see suspicious figures moving about. He crouched at the base of a wall, carefully recommencing his walk only when the street was entirely empty. It was a little before dawn when he once again slipped into the Sheikh's house. The old man was in his corner, awake and waiting for the coming call to prayer. Said took off his outer clothes and stretched out on the mat, turning his head to the wall though he had little hope of falling asleep.

"Go to sleep, for sleep is prayer for people like you," the Sheikh said.

Said made no reply. The Sheikh quickly chanted the name of God, "Allah."

When the dawn prayer was called Said was still awake and later he heard the milkman on his round. He knew he'd fallen asleep only when he was disturbed by a nightmare and opened his eyes to see light from the dim lamp spreading through the room like a fog, which made him suppose he'd slept for an hour at most. He turned toward the Sheikh's bed and found it empty, then noticed near his pile of books some cooked meat, figs, and a pitcher of water. He silently thanked the old man, wondering when he had brought the food.

Voices coming from outside the room surprised him. Creeping on all fours to the partly open door, he peeped through the crack and to his amazement saw a group of men who had come to pray, seated on mats, while a workman was busy lighting up a large oil lamp above the outer door. Suddenly he knew it was sunset, not dawn, as he had imagined.

He had slept through the whole day without realizing it, a really deep sleep indeed.

He decided to put off any further thought until after eating. He consumed the food and drank his fill, then dressed in his outdoor clothes and sat on the floor with his back against his books and his legs stretched straight out in front of him. His thoughts turned immediately to the uniform he'd forgotten, to the man who had opened the flat door to him, to Sana and Nur and Rauf and Nabawiyya and Ilish, to the informers, to Tarzan, and to the car he would use to break through the cordon. His mind churned with agitation. Clearly neither further patience nor hesitation was now in his interests. No matter what the danger, he had to contact Tarzan that night, even if it meant crawling to him over the desert sands. Tomorrow the police would be busy everywhere and those scoundrels would be out of their wits with fright.

Outside he heard someone clap his hands. The men's voices were suddenly silent and no other sounds could be heard. Sheikh Ali al-Junaydi chanted the word "Allah" three times and the others repeated the call, with a melody that brought the memory of the motion of the mystic dance to his mind once more. "Allah . . . Allah . . . Allah." The chant increased in tempo and pitch like the sound of a train racing ahead, continuing without interruption for a considerable time. Then it began gradually to lose its power, its rhythm slowing, hesitating, and finally sinking into silence. At that point a full, fine voice arose in a chanted melody:

"My time in vain is gone
And I have not succeeded.
For a meeting how I long,
But hope of peace is ended
When life is two days long;
One day of vexation
And one of separation."

Said could hear the other men murmuring sighs in appreciation all around, and then another voice began a melody:

"Love enough to lay me down enthralled:
My passion before me, my fate behind."

This song was followed by more sighs of delight and more singing, until someone clapped hands again and they all began repeating at length the name of God—Allah.

As he listened, Said allowed his mind to wander and the evening wore on. Memories came drifting by like clouds. He remembered how his father, Amm Mahran, had swayed with the chanters, while he, then a young boy, had sat near the palm tree observing the scene wide-eyed. From the shadows emerged fancies about the immortal soul, living under the protection of the Most Compassionate. Memories of hopes once bright shook off the dust of oblivion and flashed with life again: beneath that lone tree at the edge of the field tender words were whispered again in early-morning joy; little Sana sat again in his arms, speaking her first wonderful baby words. Then hot winds blew from the depths of hell and a succession of blows were struck.

In the background the prayer leader's chant and the congregation's sighs wailed on. When would peace come, when his time had passed in futility, when he had failed and fate was on his trail? But that revolver of his lying ready in his pocket, that was something at least. It could still triumph over betrayal and corruption. For the first time the thief would give chase to the dogs.

Suddenly from beneath the window outside he heard an angry voice explode and a conversation:

"What a mess! Why, the whole quarter is blocked off!"

"It's worse than during the war!"

"That Said Mahran . . . !"

Said tensed, electrified, gripping the revolver so tightly that every muscle in his body strained. He stared in every direction. The area was crowded with people and was no doubt full of eager detectives. *I mustn't let things get ahead of me. They must now be examining the uniform and the dogs will be there too. And meanwhile here I am, exposed. The desert road isn't safe, but the Valley of Death itself is only a few steps away. I can fight them there to the death.*

He got up and moved decisively toward the door. They were still engrossed in chanted prayers; the passage to the outer door was clear. He crept out into the street, then turned off to the left, walking with studied calm, moving into the road to the cemetery.

The night was well advanced, but there was no moon and the darkness made a black wall across his path. He plunged off among the tombs, into the maze of ruins, with nothing to guide him, stumbling as he walked, not knowing whether he was progressing forward or backward. Though no spark of hope glimmered within him, he felt he was bursting with incredible energy. The loud noises which were brought to him now on the warm wind made him wish he could hide inside a grave, but he knew he could not stop. He feared the dogs, but there was nothing at all he could do. There was nothing within his power to stop.

After some minutes he found himself at the last row of graves in front of a familiar scene: the northern entrance to the cemetery, connecting with Sharia Najm al-Din, which he recognized, and there the only building on it, was Nur's flat. He located the window. It was open and light was streaming out. He focused his gaze on it and saw a woman through the window. The features of her head were indistinct, but the shape of the head reminded him of Nur. His heart pumped hard at the thought. Had Nur returned, then? Or were his eyes deceiving him now, as his emotions had done before? The fact that he had become so completely deceived foretold that the end was near. If that was Nur, he told himself, all he wanted was for her to care for Sana, if his time indeed had come. He decided to shout to her, disregarding the danger, to tell her what he wanted, but before a sound could emerge from his mouth he heard dogs beginning to bark in the distance, and the barking went on, breaking the silence like a series of explosive shots.

Said started back in fright, darting in again between the tombs as the barking grew louder. He pressed his back against a tomb and took out his gun, staring out into the darkness resignedly. There it was. The dogs had come at last and there was no hope left. The scoundrels were safe, if only for a while. His life had made its last utterance, saying that it had all been in vain.

It was impossible to tell precisely where the barking came from; it was carried in on the air from all around. It was hopeless now to think of fleeing from the dark by running away into the dark. The scoundrels had indeed got away with it; his life was a proven failure. The barking and the commotion were very close now, and soon, Said knew, all the malice and vengefulness he'd been running from would be breathed right into his face. He held his gun poised as the barking grew ever louder and closer. And suddenly there was blinding light over the whole area. He shut his eyes and crouched at the base of the tomb.

"Give yourself up," a triumphant voice shouted. "It's no use resisting."

The ground shook now with the thud of heavy feet

surrounding him and the light spread all around, like the sun.

"Give yourself up, Said," the voice said firmly.

He crouched closer still to the tomb, ready to open fire, turning his head in all directions.

"Surrender," came another shout, confident, reassuring, and dignified, "and I promise you you'll be treated with all humanity."

Like the humanity of Rauf, Nabawiyya, Ilish, and the dogs no doubt? "You're surrounded on all sides. The whole cemetery is surrounded. Think it over carefully, Said. Give yourself up."

Sure that the enormous and irregular multitude of the tombs prevented them from actually seeing him, Said made no movement. He had decided on death.

"Can't you see there's no point in resistance?" the firm voice shouted.

It seemed to be nearer now than before, and Said shouted back warningly, "Any closer and I'll shoot!"

"Very well, then. What do you want to do? Make your choice between death and coming to justice."

"Justice indeed!" Said yelled scornfully.

"You're being very stubborn. You've got one minute more."

His fear-tortured eyes could see the phantom of death now, stalking through the dark.

Sana had turned away from him in alarm, hopelessly.

He sensed surreptitious movement nearby, flared with rage, and opened fire. The bullets showered in, their whistle filling his ears, chips flying from tombs all around. He fired again, oblivious to danger now, and more bullets pelted in. "You dogs, you!" he raved in a frenzy of rage, and more shots came in from all sides.

Suddenly the blinding light went out, and the firing stopped; there was darkness again and quiet fell. He wasn't firing anymore either. Slowly the silence was spreading, until all the world seemed gripped in a strange stupefaction. He wondered . . . ? But the question and even its subject seemed to dissolve, leaving no traces. Perhaps, he thought, they had retreated, slipped away into the night. Why, then, he must have won!

The darkness was thicker now and he could see nothing at all, not even the outlines of the tombs, as if nothing wished to be seen. He was slipping away into endless depths, not knowing either position, place, or purpose. As hard as he could, he tried to gain control of something, no matter what. To exert one last act of resistance. To capture one last recalcitrant memory. But finally, because he had to succumb, and not caring, he surrendered. Not caring at all now.

ALSO BY NAGUIB MAHFOUZ

CHILDREN OF THE ALLEY

The tumultuous "alley" of this rich and intricate novel (first published in Arabic in 1959) tells the story of a delightful Egyptian family, but also reveals a second, hidden, and daring narrative: the spiritual history of humankind. From the supreme feudal lord who disowns one son for diabolical pride and puts another to the test, to the savior of a succeeding generation who frees his people from bondage, we find the men and women of a modern Cairo neighborhood unwittingly reenacting the lives of their holy ancestors: the "children of the alley."

Fiction/Literature/978-0-385-26473-0

ALSO AVAILABLE

Adrift on the Nile, 978-0-385-42333-5
Akhenaten, 978-0-385-49909-5
Arabian Nights and Days, 978-0-385-46901-2
The Beggar, The Thief and the Dogs, Autumn Quail, 978-0-385-49835-7
The Beginning and the End, 978-0-385-26458-7
The Day the Leader Was Killed, 978-0-385-49922-4
Echoes of an Autobiography, 978-0-385-48556-2
The Harafish, 978-0-385-42335-9
The Journey of Ibn Fattouma, 978-0-385-42334-2
Khufu's Wisdom, 978-1-4000-7667-3
Midaq Alley, 978-0-385-26476-1
Miramar, 978-0-385-26478-5
Palace of Desire, 978-0-385-26468-6
Palace Walk, 978-0-385-26466-2
Respected Sir, Wedding Song, The Search, 978-0-385-49836-4
Rhadopis of Nubia, 978-1-4000-7668-0
The Seventh Heaven, 978-0-307-27714-5
Sugar Street, 978-0-385-26470-9
Thebes at War, 978-1-4000-7669-7
The Time and the Place, 978-0-385-26472-3
Voices from the Other World, 978-1-4000-7666-6

re, or

:om